DECEPTION IN THE BITTERROOT

IN THE

Book 2

S.S. DUSKEY

Printed in the United States of America.
First printing, 2021
Cover images by D. Driggers
Cover design and author photo by D. Driggers
Editor- Carrie Padgett
Publishing Coordinator- Sharon Kizziah-Holmes

SakiRose Publishing
Hamilton, MT

ssduskey@yahoo.com
www.ssduskeyauthor.com

ISBN- 13:978-0-578-84700-9

DEDICATION

This book is dedicated to cancer warriors: Tammy, Randi, Martha and too many others to name. Keep up the good fight and never give up hope.

ACKNOWLEDGMENTS

I would like to thank Steve Weinstock, Jon Eubanks, Charisse Rose, Teri Albrecht, D. Driggers, and John J. Alvarez, for their expertise in their respective fields.

A special note of appreciation to Ravalli County Sheriff Steve Holton, Stevensville Airport, and the staff at the Ravalli County Airport: Herman Hill and Susan Serafin.

CHAPTER 1

*B*OOM! SNAP! Lightning cracked across the gun-powder black skies. *One ... two ... three ...* I flinched and clutched my chest as the sky bellowed.

Three seconds later and another streak of light flashed, but this time a silhouette swiftly moved on the street below my office. I held my breath and bolted to the second-floor corner window, my face flush against the glass.

The figure stirred again, or so I thought. I jumped back and let out a gust of air. When I realized it was only a fallen tree branch battering the sidewalk, I lowered my shoulders and resumed scanning the streets. My gut told me he was out there, waiting like a falcon stalking its prey. Why? And who was he?

Out of nowhere, someone banged on my

door. My heart pounded and I spun.

"Whoa, sorry, Agent O'Brien. Just wanted to say goodnight." My new boss raised his hands to me. "I didn't mean to scare you." He shot me a smug grin.

"Oh, you didn't." I furrowed my brows and crossed my arms. "All good." I nodded. After he left, I rolled my eyes and resisted the urge to give him the middle finger.

After being reassigned to Headquarters, five p.m. became my favorite time of the day. I snagged my shoulder bag and black 5.11 tactical rain jacket from the hook. As I slammed the office door shut, I shimmied into my coat and dashed downstairs, taking two steps at a time. At five foot eight inches and legs to my ears, it's not difficult.

The instant I entered the lobby, my stomach flipped.

"Okay, Rose, you got this," I muttered under my breath. "If he follows me again, I will be rea—my gun, where is it!?" I fumbled through my bag and ... *Crap*, mental slap to the forehead. In my haste this morning, I left it at home.

What was I thinking? That's been one of my problems, I wasn't, and my head had not been in the game. I was somewhere in right field. Hell, who was I kidding? I wasn't even in the same stadium.

As I continued to berate myself, I flipped the hood up and darted out the door. The second my boots hit the sidewalk, I scanned left and then a rapid right. Hmm, no sign of him.

Maybe the rain scared him?

Another boom shot straight above me and the skies opened. Buckets of rain fell.

I took wide strides down First Street toward my car. Another perk of being trapped in downtown Sacramento, remote parking.

The light turned red before I made it to the intersection and I got caught waiting on the sidewalk as commuter traffic rumbled past me, soaking my new work slacks. If I were still in the field, I'd have on jeans or tactical pants and it wouldn't have mattered. My eye twitched at the injustice of it all.

As I pressed the walk button, a garbage truck turned the corner and hit a water-filled pothole. I jumped back. "Thanks ass wipe," I yelled, shook my fist, and glared at him as he passed. I could have sworn he did it on purpose.

I returned my attention to the streetlight and froze.

Out of the corner of my eye, I spied him across the street, parallel to me.

CHAPTER 2

I whirled to get a visual on him, but he leaned on his shopping cart and stuck his head in the trash bin. Probably dumpster diving. He wore dirty denim holey jeans, with a black plastic poncho tied to his waist with twine. Why would a homeless person follow me for a week? The hairs on the back of my neck stood on end. Did I know him? He didn't look familiar.

He stood greater than six feet and carried a strong limp. But where his left hand should have been, was a hook. Great. Freaking Captain Hook stalked me.

"Okay, he didn't see you. Play it cool, Rose," I muttered. "Let him follow you." I spoke to myself like a crazed street urchin.

Two days ago, a local beat cop I once worked

with stopped him and conducted a records check. The man didn't have any ID, and the name he gave wasn't known local nor did he have any warrants or criminal history. My buddy dismissed him as another lost soul roaming the streets of Sacramento. Since there wasn't any reason to bring him in, he let the vagrant go.

Tonight, I would solve the mystery. Or so I hoped.

I stood at the corner repeatedly pressing the *Walk* button and tapping one leg, waiting for permission to cross. Once it changed green, I sped to the other side and zipped down State Street.

He followed suit. But for someone with a hobble, he gained on me. The thumping of his shopping cart grew louder and the roar of the cars zooming past magnified in my brain. I wanted with every ounce of my being to pounce on his ass, but there were too many witnesses.

Since I was recently given a written letter of instruction over a public and heated conversation with my boss, I didn't want to take any chances, so I lured him away from the public eye.

There was my chance. I took a sharp right and shrank into the alley between State and Second. My heart palpitated and for a cool rainy October day, I sweated .223 bullets. The smell of the first rain in months emitted from the asphalt and the droplets fell against my coat, beading onto my face. If I weren't in secret psycho-squirrel mode, I would have relished the moment.

As his steps drew closer, he murmured something inaudible, and the clanking of his shopping cart disappeared. He must've ditched it.

I stood with gritted teeth, clenched fists, and a bladed stance. The second he rounded the corner, I clothes-lined him. It wasn't a technique taught in the academy, but what's another reprimand?

"Argh." I winced as an intense shooting pain radiated through my left shoulder. I immediately regretted not using my right. During the adrenaline surge, I'd forgotten about my recent gunshot wound.

The force of my blow knocked him on his back. He landed on three filled and soaked black garbage bags from the Chinese restaurant. Discarded egg rolls and noodles cushioned his fall.

As my stalker lay face up, his features faded to the shadows of the alley and his arms flailed around like a turtle flipped on its back.

There was something different. Wait! Where was his hook? It occurred to me both of this fellow's limbs were intact. I stood ready for a fight that never happened.

He laid on the ground and didn't jump up as I expected. He screamed, "What the *hell*, Rose?"

Just then an oncoming car headlight shone, illuminating his face.

I knew him.

"Ah crap!" I blurted.

CHAPTER 3

"**W**hat the hell is wrong with you?" James bellowed.

I stared with a gaped mouth at my former work partner and best friend, James Powers, or as I fondly referred to him as the goofy character, Austin Powers, AP for short. He called me Felicity in his jollier moments. This wasn't one of them.

I reached out a hand.

James's brown eyes narrowed, and his mouth hardened. "No, thanks, *Agent O'Brien*. You might zonk me again. Or worse yet, shoot me!"

"Nah, left it at home." I snarked.

James bolted to his feet as the back-alley light went on. He pinched his lips and glared at me as he removed the noodles from his black,

FBI logo-embossed jacket. He shook his soaked chestnut brown hair draping his brows.

"Hey, I'm so sorry, AP, but that homeless dude I told you about was following me again. You know, the one with the limp and the hook." I held my left hand like a claw.

By the silence that hung in the air, James wasn't in the mood for my sarcasm.

I exhaled and shook my head. "Anyway, I thought you were him, with the limp and all ... hey what's up with that?" I glanced at his leg.

"I was fine a few minutes ago. I called out for you, but you didn't answer. You were in a zone and kept looking back. I figured today's meeting didn't go well." He rubbed his inner thigh. "And I may have pulled a groin muscle chasing you ... so what happened?"

"First, I can kiss off any hopes of returning to the field. It's worse. They think I'm a loose cannon and bad news for the department. Not to mention they're still sore at me for omitting the truth from my background. But they can't hold that over me." I clenched my teeth. "It's not my fault they changed our names, I was just a kid. I wasn't allowed to tell anyone ... even you." I lowered my gaze. "It's another excuse. They're gunning for me and want me gone. And get this, they set me up to see a freakin' Employee Assistance Program shrink! Screw th—"

Bang! Shots rang out.

I crouched in the alley with my hands over my head. "Get down!" I cried, my heart in my throat, a tremble working its way up my legs into my arms, my chest, my throat until I couldn't breathe.

James bit his lip and stared at me with soft eyes. "Love, it's just a car backfiring." He grabbed my elbow. "Felicity, maybe that EAP doc is not such a bad ide—"

"Not you too, AP!" I shot to my feet and yanked my arm away. "You're supposed to be on my team, *partner*. Forget them, and ... you too."

We locked eyes for a second.

I shook my head and stormed off, leaving James in the alley with the old egg rolls.

CHAPTER 4

"**W**elcome home, Husband." Saki threw herself into his arms the second James opened the apartment door. Her long, blonde cascading locks covered his broad chest. She stood on tiptoes and planted a lingering kiss on him. At five-five, she stood five inches shorter than him.

"It's only been a month and I love how your blue eyes twinkle every time you call me, *husband.*" He set his FBI duffle bag on the floor and wiggled out of his coat.

"O.M.G., you're soaked, and you smell like egg foo young." Saki removed food particles from his mustache. "What the hell happened? Did you tackle a bad guy in a Chinese restaurant?" She giggled as she took his jacket to the laundry room.

James went into the bathroom and turned on the shower as he recapped his encounter with Rose.

"Holy, shit! My sister did that to you? I am so sorry." Saki followed him and plopped on the vanity sink.

"It's not your fault. I'm concerned about her, she needs to see someone. She hasn't been the same since we returned from Florida," James replied.

"I'm worried too. Now that we're married, she thinks I don't need her anymore. Ugh, wait until she finds out we're moving ... don't assume you told her?" Saki shrugged her shoulders and squinted. She regretted it the instant she said it.

"Seriously, Babe?" James popped his head from behind the shower curtain. "Not a chance. I was glad she left her gun at home today."

"She what?! Rose *never* leaves that thing ... it's like her right arm." Saki jumped off the sink and handed James a towel. "Oh, shit! This is serious. Maybe she just needs some time off ... speaking of a vacation." Saki made her way to the living room and sat on the couch. She scrolled through her phone. "I got a text message from Kevin today."

"Kevin O'Malley from Miami? What did he say?" James emerged from the bathroom in a robe and with a towel around his neck. He plopped next to Saki.

"Other than giving me the contact for the Bureau's re-locators, he was offered an all-expenses paid trip to Montana. Something about fishing and hunting. But we leave Friday, that's in three days." Saki handed James the phone.

"Hmm ... first-class travel and a kick-ass lodge. Meals included. That sounds perfect. I've got a week coming to me. They said anytime. Besides, with my transfer, they already have my position filled." He raised his brows.

"Um, Babe. Do you think we can invite Rose?" Saki wrinkled her nose. "I know he has a thing for her, and she rejected him. But ... I don't want to leave her. She needs a break."

"I'll ask Kevin. And you're right, a vacation will do her good. At least there's no swamps in Montana." James chuckled.

"Not funny, Mr. Powers. You were almost crocodile food." Saki interlaced her hand with his. "Hey, if we're inviting Rose, how about Kaylee? It would give me a chance to get to know my half-sister." Saki's voice went up like a child's. "Kevin said, 'the more the merrier.'" She eased her head on his shoulder and flickered her eyelashes.

"Okay, Mrs. Powers. I can't resist your azure blues. I will text your stubborn sister and double check with Kevin about Kaylee. Fresh air and nature. Hmm. What could go wrong?"

CHAPTER 5

I glared at the sign. *Dr. R. Brody, Ph.D.*, read the name on the window to hell. Her office sat in the heart of Midtown, right off Broadview Street. It was in a single story, red brick building with two other suites: an orthodontist and physical therapist.

I'd thought the address looked familiar. I'd spent three and a half months undergoing rigorous PT. Being shot in the shoulder and having it repeatedly torn takes a toll on a gal. Not to mention my shredded Achilles from the boat dock explosion. But I never paid attention to any of the other offices in the building, until now.

The second I opened the door, lavender essential oils misted the air. The waiting room had soft tones and self-help magazines displayed in monthly order on the table. Ocean waves played. I looked around and noted I was the only sucker in the room.

"Good Morning, Rose. I'm ready for you." A woman greeted me with a warm smile and a firm handshake. There was a youthfulness about her, but by the dates of the certificates on the wall, Dr. Brody should have been in her late sixties.

"My name is Dr. Lane, but you can call me Shilo." She was striking, with light brown hair and round hazel eyes hidden behind wire-rimmed Gucci glasses. Dr. Lane wore ankle-high black boots, black leggings, and a red-plaid jacket that hung just below her bottom.

We met at the same height and weight.

"What happened to Dr. Brody?" I squinted.

"Uh ... she is not available, I took over the practice. I haven't had the chance to make the change on the door."

"Oh, okay. I wish I were told that, I already researched her. I don't know anything about you." I crossed my arms.

"I assure you, I'm quite capable." She shot a closed mouth smile. "Please come in and take a seat, Rose. May I call you that?" Shilo motioned to a black leather loveseat across from her matching recliner chair. She grabbed a cell phone off her brown leather top antique Sligh desk.

I nodded and sat.

"Do you mind?" She snapped a photo. "I like to have a picture of my clients ... you know for their files and all."

I pulled my head back and furrowed my brows.

"Please put your purse down and relax."

My 'purse' as she called it was a gift from my late husband, Bradley. A black and brown concealed carry crossbody bag. My 9 mm M&P Shield fit perfectly in it. I wasn't about to leave it behind again. I held it close to me.

"So, tell me Rose, what brings you in today?" she asked with a warm smile and sincere tone.

"Well, other than my incident with my ex-partner, uh-er brother-in-law yesterday, my department thinks I'm crazy." I exhaled an exaggerated sigh.

"We in the field prefer not to use that term," Shilo said.

"Yeah, yeah. I minored in psychology. Okay … they think I'm unhinged. Is that better? They removed me from the streets and placed me on a temporary assignment to headquarters so they could babysit me." I tapped my feet on the floor like an anxious puppy and looked around the room. "But I don't need a sitter … I'm *fine*."

She looked at me over the top of her glasses.

"No, I am not f'd-up, neurotic, and emotional, fine. I am okay … I … I'm good."

"All right. I see here you were involved in a few incidences." She flipped through pages in her file. "You were shot in the line of duty? And within the span of a week, you shot three peop—"

"Four." I mumbled as I stared at my dry cuticles. "Excluding the crocodile." I looked up and faked a smile. "But he was chomping my partner and another dirt bag in the swamps of the Florida Keys."

"Okay ... four," Shilo said in a slow and hesitant manner as she crossed her legs. "But none were fatal? Uh ... except the crocodile?" she asked in a higher pitch.

"No. My parolee, Jessie. But my shot was not the kill shot. His head was blown off first, by the dirtbag from the swamp I just mentioned. Who by the way was eaten by the croc. Soo ... that makes two dead," I said as if I were ordering a pizza with extra toppings.

"Rose, how does this make you feel?"

"Fine. I mean, how would it make you feel? It was all justified. They cleared me of any wrongdoing." I let out an enormous yawn.

"This is about you, not me. And I don't know you well, but you have dark circles under your eyes as if you haven't slept in a month. Am I correct? And how is yo—"

"I'll save you the mental status eval." I raised my hand to her. "I am not a danger to others, gravely disabled, nor do I want to eat my own gun." I counted on my fingers and sat forward in my seat.

"Um ... that is good to know." She cleared her throat. "Rose, do you consume alcohol?" She interlaced her fingers and tipped her head to the side.

"Barely. But maybe a couple glasses of wine at night. Just enough for me to relax. It buys me about four hours of sleep. Look—" I stood and kicked my chair from behind me. "I don't wake up drinking, nor do I have one stashed in my office drawer. Although that would make my desk job more bearable." I growled.

Shilo let out a puff of air. "Let's talk about something else." She motioned for me to sit.

"No, thanks, I've heard it's worse than smoking. For your health, you know. Too much sitting." I shuffled the length of her office and ran my fingers over the psychology books on the shelf.

"Okay. Standing is acceptable too. I see in your file, there have been a couple recent deaths in your family. Have you worked through any of this ... you know, had any closure?"

"Closure is overrated." I continued perusing the books.

"Let me ask you something."

"Yeah?" I turned back to her.

"Do you always wear armor?"

I peered down at my chest. "I'm not wearing my ballistic vest. What are you talking about?" I curled my lip.

"I meant metaphorically. You've got shields up and you wear it around here." She patted her chest. "You have a bit of a superhero complex too. Not to mention you use anger and sarcasm as a defense mechanism. And the most recent events just piled it on you. It can cause irritability and jumpiness. Also known as Post—"

"Don't ... don't say that word. I don't have it. And I'm glad you psychoanalyzed me so fast!" I barked and turned away.

"Well, it's more common than you think,

especially with law enforcement officers and military. Trust me, I understand. Your body's alarm system has been compromised and needs to be re-programmed." She put her pen down and interlaced her fingers. "So, tell me about your husband, um ... Bradley. You lost him sev—"

"*Lost?*" I yelled and snapped my head back to her, giving myself whiplash. "Losing someone indicates you may find them again. *No*! Bradley was murdered," I said with gritted teeth and slammed my hands on the back of the chair, shooting daggers at her.

"Okay, Rose." She put her hands up as if she were slowing me down. "Anger is a part of the healing process, and two people close to you died within the span of a year. Your mother and husband. You need to allow yourself to mourn and grieve these los—uh, deaths. When was the last time you took a vacation?" she asked calmly.

Vacation? That was random. I turned and made my way to the window as tears formed behind my eyes, twirling my silver wedding band around my finger. *Don't lose it, Rose.* I drew a deep breath.

"Look. I've seen my share over in Afghanistan. So, I get it. Um ... would you like a glass of water?" Shilo asked as she stepped behind her desk and poured from a decanter on her credenza.

I nodded and stared into the street as I opened the window. "I have mostly good days. But everyone thinks I'm cr ... uh ..." I peered over my shoulder at her. "Imagining things. But there's a guy who I think ... no, I know, has been following me."

A cool fall breeze blew in the room. I drew a deep breath and closed my eyes.

When I opened them, he stood across the street, staring at me.

CHAPTER 6

Although he got paid to follow her, the hook man relished it. The revenge tasted like honey whiskey on his lips, and he wanted her to feel his presence. After all, Rose was the cause of his disfigurement.

"Do you have eyes on her?" the man on the other end of the phone snapped.

"Yup, your red-headed beauty walked into that shrink's office a few minutes ago." The disheveled street man replied with a strong Bronx accent.

"Don't get too close, she can't recognize ... not yet."

"Fat chance ... and do *not* tell me how to handle this situation, or her, Thomas, or whatever the fuck you're called now," he shouted.

"Excuse me! Do I need to remind you who is backing your little adventure?" Thomas retorted.

"Yeah, yeah ... when I'm done wit' her, she is gonna be begging for a vacation or wish she were never born."

A glass clinked on the other end of the line.

"It's ten o'clock in the morning, already drinking, Thomas?"

"It's none of your freaking business. I'm halfway around the world. But yes." Thomas let out an exaggerated sigh. "I'm in my spa overlooking the Turquoise Sea. Haven't you forgotten, I'm persona non grata in the States?"

"Perfect! I'm freezing my ass off on the streets and you're playing rub a dub dub. Ya probably got half naked twins wit' ya."

"Well, not twins. They're American models in Italy doing a show."

He heard what sounded like women giggling and the splashing of water.

"That's nice." He seethed through gritted teeth as he leaned on his shopping cart.

"Screw you. You're doing this for yourself, too. Besides, you'd be dead if I didn't find you," Thomas snapped.

"I wouldn't have been in *that* situation to begin with if it weren't for *you* and Rose. So, what are your plans for her?"

"I want what belongs to me." Thomas sneered.

"You got a sick obsession with her, it's not healthy."

"So is arguing with the person who could

and should have let you die," Thomas said.

The hook man pulled the phone away from his ear and furrowed his brows. His rage brewed. But for now, he needed to play it cool for his former boss. He had a plan of his own.

"Hey, gotta go. She spotted me." He ended the call.

CHAPTER 7

Hook Man stood across the street leaning on his shopping cart, talking on a cell. He eyed me a brief moment, then hung up. He wore the same black poncho with a camouflage Boonie hat. His shoulder length hair was brown and scraggly and his beard matched. Black, thick framed sunglasses concealed his eyes.

"Who the hell are you?" I pounded on the window frame as I shouted through the screen.

"Excuse me, Rose?" Shilo snapped.

"You son of a bitch," I hollered, then bolted out the office door and to the corner.

Broadview is a major street in Midtown with a two-lane opposing roadway. I stood a mere two-hundred feet away and had better visual on him.

"What the freak do you want?" I flailed my hands in the air and shouted until the veins protruded from my neck.

The creep didn't respond. He stood with a smug grin and used his hook arm to draw a cutting motion across his neck and flipped me off with his right middle finger.

The light turned green, and I jumped off the sidewalk and bolted into the street. An approaching car slammed its brakes, and the driver shouted something obscene. The game *Frogger* came to mind as I dodged vehicles and made my way to the median strip.

The second I landed on the center island, a city bus arrived. Passengers unloaded and blocked my view. *Crap, lost sight of him.* I stepped into the roadway, but the horses were out of the gate and I couldn't make it in time.

As the bus took off, so did the jerk. He vanished along with his shopping cart.

I stood, frozen in the median as cars sped by me, blaring their horns. People stared. The world stopped around me for a second and then started again, but this time in slow-motion. A fire truck roared past me, sirens wailing. I snapped and shook my head. As I turned my back to Shilo looking out the window, she wore what appeared to be a concerned expression.

I pondered my sanity for a moment. Was I the only one who saw him? I turned to return to my appointment, but out of the corner of my eye, a neon light flashed *Open*. A bar. I ping-ponged my attention from Shilo to the tavern.

The decision was a no brainer. I crossed the street.

CHAPTER 8

My eyes felt like lead as I opened them and saw two of everything. I woke face down on the carpet, my head pounding and the worst nausea of my life roiling through my stomach. As I gingerly rolled over and gazed at the wall, my double vision dissipated, and I spotted the wedding picture of me and Bradley.

"Thank God, I'm home," I mumbled. I pushed to my knees and caught a glimpse of the time. Crap, 6:30 a.m., gonna be late for work. And then I remembered I took off a couple weeks. "Thank God, again," I muttered and crawled into the bathroom just in time to pray to the porcelain king. Heck, I did more than that, I had a full-blown conversation.

After my abdominal workout, I leaned

against the wall with my head on my knees.

"Oh boy. I figured you'd end up here." James stepped into the room and flushed the commode.

"Hi." I looked at him and muttered almost under my breath. "How did you know I'd be here?"

"Uh, Felicity ... you live here," James snarked.

"Smart ass, I meant in this condition!" I was in no mood for sarcasm unless it came from me.

"Are you all right?" He bent down and patted my head.

"Does it look like I'm all right?" I pulled away. "And I'm not a freakin' dog."

"You don't remember, do you?" He handed me a revolting looking green icy beverage from Java Hut.

"Ugh, no thanks." I held up my hand.

"You called me, slurring you needed a ride. You mumbled no one needs you anymore, the hook man is after you and some other nonsense I couldn't understand."

I crawled back to the bedroom and inched onto the bed.

"Felicity, your sister and I are worried about you."

"Pshh. I'm fine." I shrugged. "I'm good. I'm a big girl and can handle myself," I said.

"Well ... that's not all. Love. We need to talk," James replied with a lowered tone.

"AP ..." I slumped with my head in my hands. "Can the lecture wait ... oh, crap." It suddenly occurred to me. "Did Heidi see me?" I shot my eyes to the door, looking for my current roommate and once-upon-a-time caretaker and babysitter.

"Yep, she just left to buy you ginger ale. She also said something about making chicken soup."

"Jeezo, now I'm really ashamed." I drew the pillow to my face. If I could have suffocated myself, I would've.

"Felicity, that's not all you have to be embarrassed about." He plopped next to me.

"Huh?" I reared my head back. "Wait ... wait, wait. How did I get home? Where's my car? And my keys?" I scanned the room.

"First, your car is on the street and the keys are on the dining room table. My buddy Alan drove it home for you. Second, after your appointment you hit the bar. For a few hours."

"What? My appointment was over at eleven o'clock."

James stared at me and cocked his head.

"Okay, I ended it early." I let out a heavy sigh.

"I heard." He stood. "Hey, what's the last thing you remember?"

"I was yelling at someone at the bar." I shut my eyes, hoping to recover the memory from my foggy brain.

"Yeah, that would've been your new boss."

"Wha ... I did what? To whom?" My mouth hung wide.

"You got a bit of a problem." He walked into the bathroom and ran cold water over a washcloth and placed it on my forehead.

"Drinking that early was a bad idea. I thought I'd start a new hobby." I snickered. "I can certainly scratch alcoholic off my list. Come to think of it ... I'm positive I ordered coffee and not booze." I tightened my fists. "It's Shilo's fault, if only she ha—"

"That's not your problem." He stared down at me and crossed his arms.

"AP. You're doing that lip biting thing. Spill it."

"What I've been trying to tell you. Um ... you called your boss a quote, unquote, *pencil-dick, twat-waffle.*" He air quoted.

I snort-laughed. "Ow, that hurts." And gripped my head. "You know, he hasn't even earned the title of a twat—"

"It's not funny. You went viral." He pulled his phone from his back pocket and scrolled.

"Shit!" I snatched the cell and replayed the YouTube video. "Oh, they made a meme too." I stared. "I'm screwed, aren't I?"

He pursed his lips and nodded. "I got a call from one of the big wigs on the third floor, the one I play golf with. You gotta know, they're not happy with you."

I darted into the bathroom and had another conversation with the toilet.

"Here, let me get your hair out of the line of fire." James tied my mane back. "And he told me that while they do not like your *'waffle'* boss up there, he wasn't happy it was posted for all to see. Not to mention you were in a bar ... on duty." James flushed the commode again. "I reminded him you're a bit of a hero and saved my ass in Florida, and you took a bullet for the department. But he said you are a shit storm of a mess, with anger issues."

"Why does everyone say that?" I shouted and clamped my pounding head. "And I swear, James. I just ordered coffee."

"Sure, you did ... why didn't you go to a coffee shop?" James asked with his hands on his hips.

"Thought about that, but the bar was closer and taunted me. I had every intention of pounding a shot." I rubbed my face. "But ... I did not." I said, slow and deliberate. "James, you have to believe me, someone spiked it." I pounded my fists on the tile floor.

"Come here. Look at you." He helped me to my feet and stood me in front of the mirror with his hands on my shoulders. "You know how crazy that sounds? The hook man is following you. Someone spiked your coffee."

"Uh, Shilo said not to use that term." I stared at myself in the mirror. "My hair looks like I've been tasered. Hmm, that's an idea. I might feel better."

"Love. I made a call. Here's the deal. You need to stay away from your office for the rest of the week and all next. No more drunken videos and for God's sake, keep your distance from the waffle."

"I already took two weeks off ... perfect timing, huh?" I bowed my head. I couldn't look at myself anymore.

"Last thing. I agreed to keep an eye on you.

So, you *are* going to Montana with Saki and me."

"That's freaking great. You're relegated my babysitter now? And Montana? Why there?"

"My friend Kevin in Miami? He was offered a free stay at a lodge and he's invited us along."

I shook my head. "I ... need to think about it. I can maybe meet you guys there in a couple da—"

"Nut-un. Last time you pulled that stunt you ran off to the Keys ... solo."

"I promise, AP. A couple days, max." I put my little finger out. He linked it with his. "Pinky promise?" I shot him my pathetic puppy eyes.

"Okay." He sighed and rolled his eyes. He kissed my forehead. "Ick. For God's sake, take a shower and brush your damn teeth," he shouted as he marched out the door.

After James left, I washed up and fell into a long nap.

CHAPTER 9

Thomas swam morning laps in his Olympic-sized heated saltwater pool on the main floor of his tri-level, seven-bedroom, six bath Porto Cervo Villa. Although the temperature read seventeen degrees Celsius in Sardinia, warming heaters sat on each curve of his wrap-around deck. The villa had been in his family for generations and since he'd been banished from the States, it became his permanent home.

In between laps, Thomas sat under the Gallura Granite waterfall at the far end of the pool. He closed his eyes and savored the solitude as the cascades pounded him. His adventure in the Florida Keys a few months prior left an unsettling emptiness. So, Thomas did something he thought he'd never do. He'd sought counseling. He couldn't risk Sammy, the weak little boy, emerging again. Thomas spent an average person's annual income on a therapist to make sure of it. He followed the therapist's recommendation and dumped the band he wore on his wrist and took up swimming.

As he popped out of the pool, an Italian twenty-something-year-old with legs to her ears wrapped him in a warm towel. All his staff were female, with red hair. He liked them that way. Thomas went through employees like water and never bothered remembering their names. He'd snap his fingers or ring a bell, and they catered to his every whim.

Thomas lay on his oversized chaise longue and basked his chiseled one-hundred-and-eighty-pound body in the sun. He smoothed down his dyed goatee. He was going to enjoy being a blond for a while. He mused as his staff handed him a cup of Kopi Luwak coffee.

Like his java, Thomas liked his twinkies imported.

Tiffany and Shandrell, models from New York, emerged from their rooms in matching pink terry cloth robes. Shandrell, he referred to as 'the brunette,' curled up next to him on the chaise, while Tiffany, the blonde, leaned behind him with her robe open, pressing her exposed breasts against the nape of his neck.

Thomas sighed and narrowed his cerulean eyes. "Off me!" He brushed Shandrell away. Sex he enjoyed, but cuddling, not so much.

"What an ass." Shandrell snatched Thomas'

cup and sashayed to an empty chair.

Thomas snapped his fingers, and another cup sat in his hands in seconds.

"I love your views of Costa Smeralda." Tiffany massaged Thomas's scalp. "And your villa is fabulous with the tiled floors ... are the outside walls made from local granite?"

"Yes, they are. I wanted it to look authentic. I remodeled it to suit my taste." He deliberately raised his eyebrows.

"Interior design is my specialty, it is my fall back when I'm too old to model. But I have to say, I am especially fond of helicopters." Tiffany leaned over and licked his ear. "Have you ever, you know, done it in your chopper?"

He furrowed his brows as he looked at his Airbus H175 and glared back at her.

Tiffany took one long continuous breath. "Mmm, I can still smell your aftershave."

"It's my one-of-a-kind design, made here in Italy. But I am rather tired of it and have another in the making." He smirked.

"Well, whatever, it'd make my panties drop, if I wore any." She giggled and continued exploring his body. She traced her long pink acrylic nail from his neck, down his chest, to his abdomen. "Where did you get this scar? It's kinda sexy."

"Gunshot wound, I'd rather not talk about it. Now go." Thomas pushed her away, too.

"You *are* an asshole!" Tiffany huffed, grabbed the coffee from his hands and took a sip.

"Yeah, that's what I've been told." A third

cup was in his hands before he requested one. He returned his attention to the sea.

"Mmm, what's this coffee?" Shandrell asked from her perch.

"It's Kopi Luwak, digested by Palm Civet," Thomas replied.

"Huh?" Shandrell tilted her head.

"It's cat poop coffee," Tiffany snarked.

Shandrell spit out a mouthful of coffee into her cup. "What the hell? We're drinking cat shit coffee! Gads, that's disgusting."

"Yep. The cat eats the beans and poops it out, that's how they make it. I read about it. You just spit out thirty-five bucks' worth of coffee." Tiffany laughed.

"No, it's one hundred dollars." Thomas sighed.

"I don't care, it's gross." Shandrell glared at Thomas and curled her nose, shaking her head.

Thomas rolled his eyes and flicked his wrist. "You two can go now. I'm finished with you."

Tiffany stood. "No ... we're done with you. Come on, Shandrell. We're young and beautiful and don't need this crap. Besides, Cervo is a billionaire's playground, we can do better than him."

Shandrell stood and nodded at Tiffany.

They glared at Thomas and with cheeky grins dumped two-hundred dollars-worth of coffee in his spa.

Thomas shook his head and stared at the sea. His love would never do such an amateur thing.

His therapist encouraged Thomas to forget

Rose once and for all. But he could not get her out of his mind. Or his heart. Her golden, red-silky hair, flawless skin, and sapphire blue eyes would be his. She would learn to love him again. But first, he had to persuade her. And he would. By any means possible.

His cell phone interrupted his fantasy.

"Is the chopper fueled for tomo—I don't care it's less than an hour drive to Olbia. You're new … aren't you? Put Crock on the phone!" Thomas scratched his goatee and rolled his neck.

"What the hell is wrong with your cousin? You need to school him … and fast! If we weren't leaving tomorrow and the documents already submitted to Customs, Dale would be out. I don't have time to find a second pilot, I'll need two of you in Montana. Oh, and by the way, we're not flying to Hamilton. We're going to stay at the lake house in Whitefish … I have a business meeting. Besides, the lodge is occupied." He smirked and ended the call and returned his attention to the ocean, sipping his Luwak.

CHAPTER 10

I woke up at noon to the smell of chicken soup. I sat up in bed and looked down. I wore my superhero jammies. I didn't remember putting those on. Sheesh, I was more messed up than I thought. The entire morning was a blur. Was it a dream? As of late, dreams and reality seemed more and more muddled.

I spotted the empty beverage container on my nightstand. It hit me, I could lose my job. But I still didn't remember consuming alcohol or saying those things. I was never that reckless.

As I rolled over, the aroma from the kitchen intensified and for the first time in months a smile almost crept to the corners of my mouth. *Thank you, Heidi Zimm.* I don't know what I would've done without her.

Heidi moved in with me when we returned from Florida and she nursed me back to health. She stayed and never looked back. After all, she needed a break after leaving that *waffle*—my new favorite word—Max. Ugh, the mere mention of his name made me want to have one last conversation with the toilet, but I resisted.

I contemplated getting up, until I heard a gentle rap at the door.

"Good afternoon, Rosie," Heidi crooned. She came in carrying a tray with homemade chicken soup, crackers, and ginger ale.

"Hi, you're a gem. You know I'm not sick." I snickered.

"Well, dear, not from what I heard earlier," she said.

Saki was right. Heidi did sound like Saki's childhood Mrs. Beasley doll.

"I don't deserve you." I reached for the tray.

"Oh, your mother would disagree about that." Heidi sang as she took the Java Hut cup and washcloth from my nightstand. After so many years caring for the psychopath, I think she enjoyed the more lowkey craziness that followed me.

I winced as I sat and yanked on my hair, squeezing my eyes. A vice-grip constricted my head, or so it felt.

"You need an aspirin?"

"Yes, please." I rubbed my forehead. "Oh, sorry. It's in my car in the center console." I threw my feet over the bed. "I'll get th—"

"No, you don't, young lady. Let me." She pushed me back.

"Heidi, thank you. The keys are on the dining room table. You're an angel. Hey, I got an idea. Will you come to Montana with us? It'll be a nice, relaxing trip. And you are a huge part of our family again." I titled my head and gave her my best puppy dog eyes.

"Let me think about that, I'll be right back." She beamed.

I blew her a kiss.

She padded down the hall and opened the front door. An odd chirping of my key fob came next.

"Hmm, the battery must be going de—" My thoughts were interrupted by an intense shaking of my house followed by a loud *boom*!

I tossed my tray onto the bed, bolted up, and darted to my bedroom window. Pieces of my Toyota Highlander sailed through the air.

"Heidi!" I sprinted to the front door. My heart walloped.

CHAPTER 11

"**H**ey! Do you have someone else working out here?" Hook Man seethed in a low voice through gritted teeth as he sat at the airport bar.

"Hmm? Wha?" A yawn came from the other end of the call.

"Her car blew up. I'm watching the news coverage now. An explosion or some shit. I didn't do it." He took a shot of Patron Silver.

"It's two a.m. This better be a bloody dream or you're dead," Thomas snapped.

"Not in California it's not and I don't care. This is important." He put his hand over the phone.

"Where are you?"

"I'm headed back to Mon—uh, Miami, remember. Answer the question. Was this your job?" He yelled as his face grew hot with anger.

"First, don't *ever* raise your voice to me. You're lucky you're still above ground. Second, not my work ... are you drinking?" Thomas spoke in a low and controlled tone, which Hook Man knew was more dangerous than a shout.

"Yeah, so what. You try flying with half your body full of metal shit and see how you like it. Besides, you don't own me anymore," he shouted.

Patrons in the lounge stopped their conversations and stared.

The bartender touched her finger to her lips and shook her head.

"You know, maybe it wasn't a hit, and it just exploded. Crap like that happens. Or—"

"Or maybe a freaking unicorn will come sliding down a double rainbow licking an ice cream cone ... *of course* it's a hit." Thomas seethed.

"This might alter her plans. But whether she goes or not, I did my part and expect to get paid." He put his finger up to the bartender for another round.

"Trust me, she'll go." Thomas yawned again. "And I already transferred your money, but if you continue to tell me what to do, I can take it back."

The hook man pulled the cell away from his ear, knocked back one more shot, and ended the call. "Asshole," he screamed at the phone.

The conversations stopped again, and people gawked with open mouths.

"What the fuck you all looking at?" He

slammed cash on the bar and stormed out, flailing his hook.

He paced the airport terminal, waiting for his flight. He despised flying, especially with a prosthetic arm and leg. He was a freak show going through security. They took swabs all around his fake appendages to detect bomb-making material before ushering him to a private screening room. He drank to calm his nerves.

"Attention passengers, this is your final boarding announcement," an airline gate attendant cheerfully announced over the loudspeaker.

He limped to Gate A as he glanced at his bank transfer.

Hmm, tight ass. He deserved a lot more for all the shit he went through ... and he'd get it too. He might even be able to afford real prosthetics. He smirked as he used his hook to give the attendant the boarding pass to Missoula.

CHAPTER 12

"I'm sorry, Heidi, it's all my fault." I leaned over and kissed her forehead as the paramedics covered her with a blanket. "I swear, I'm gonna find the person responsible and deal with them, if it's the last thing I do." I spoke through tears and gnashed teeth.

My sleepy Grass Valley rural neighborhood rattled and rolled that afternoon. Trouble had a way of following me. I looked to the heavens. God, what did I do to deserve this? Was it because I didn't go to church anymore?

My discussion with the Creator was interrupted when James arrived. He stopped his G ride short and angled it between the paramedics and fire truck. His red and blue emergency lights flashed in the grill. He jumped out, presented his badge, and ducked under the yellow crime scene tape.

"How'd you get here so fast?" I squinted and hugged myself to keep the chill away.

"I was finishing a case in the county and heard the call over the radio." He touched my arm. "How is she? Is she de—"

Out of nowhere, a sputter sounded followed by tapping then a loud boom. We all flinched, including the emergency personnel.

It was Saki. She jerked her Toyota into the driveway and as she turned it off, it sounded like another explosion.

"Too bad her car isn't in pieces. She could use a new one." I mocked.

"Rosie." She ran into my arms, sobbing. "Are you okay? Is Heidi all right?"

"See for yourself, honey." I shot my eyes to the ambulance.

Saki nodded with tears flowing down her face and rushed to Heidi.

I bent over and dry heaved on the ground. I felt as if someone punched me in the stomach.

"We all have an expiration date." I stood. "Thank God today is not Heidi's. She had a guardian angel watching over her. The blast wave pushed her back in the house. She must've unlocked the Highlander's doors with my key fob from behind the security screen. She's gonna be bruised and have ringing in her ears for a while." I turned to James. "It's a good thing I installed that screen after Titos bashed in my front door ... anyway, the paramedics are transporting her to the hospital to check for any internal damage. But she's a resilient sixty-four-year-old," I said.

"Yes, she is ... sooo, you think your vehicle blowing up will take the heat off your problems?" He sneered.

"Not funny, James. You don't think ..." I looked around, leaned in, and whispered. "He had anything to do with it?"

"Max? Hmm, I wouldn't put it past him. As far as I know, he's still out of the country. There's been no chatter of his name or attempt to re-enter," James replied.

"And to answer your question, AP, no! This won't take the *heat* off me. I'll phone my supervisor later." I rolled my eyes. "Well, maybe his boss."

"They'll be contacting you soon. I took the luxury of making the call. And you know they'll conduct a threat assessment."

"Yep, I've been down this road." I sighed.

Saki returned to us. "Holy shit, sis, you're lucky. And so is Heidi. But your car, not so much." She stared at the metal remains of my SUV. "Oh ... I have a message. Heidi would love to go to Montana. I guess almost getting blown to smithereens makes a person wanna get away."

Saki turned her attention to James and put her head on his shoulder. "Now more than ever I think we all need to get aw—" Saki's phone rang. "It's Kaylee." She stepped aside to take the call.

"Well ..." James picked up my license plate and examined it. "Since you already took off a couple weeks."

"What about the investigation?" I dropped my head into my hands.

"The lead investigator, Jon, is a friend of mine, and he'll keep me in the loop. Besides, you may be safer away from all this until the investigation is complete." He handed me my plate. "They're canvassing your 'hood right now. It's a good thing your neighbors are so far apart, no need to evacuate. But they're still knocking on doors to check on folks. Oh, they'll want your security footage," James said.

"I already gave Jon my statement. And before I hand over the surveillance tape, I'm gonna watch it first."

"I wouldn't expect anything less." He shot me a closed mouth grin and cocked his head to the side. "Let me know if you see anything."

Saki returned. "Kaylee's all in, she'll talk to you later, Rose. I guess you were going to help her move back to Florida?" She raised her brows.

I nodded. "It's a long story. She's leaving her residency program and returning home. Tubbs is flying in tomorrow. I'll fill you in later."

"That's perfect. Rose and Heidi will hitch a ride, and we can still make our first-class flight tomorrow morning." Saki shot wide, cheeky glances between James and me.

"I'm not sure." I threw my palms up and looked away. "My car just blew up, it's kind of a game changer. And I've got so much shit going on here."

Saki stared with a gaped mouth.

"I guess I rubbed off on you, sis. Now you have potty mouth." Saki smirked.

I flashed her a sideways glare. I was in no mood for a lecture about manners from anyone.

"Come on, it will be good for you and you promised earlier." James pulled up a pinky finger.

"Yeah, that was before … having my car blown up negates the pinky swear, so we'll see. For now, I'll take Heidi's Audi and follow her to the hospital."

"Uh … not in those, Rose. You need to fix yourself, you look like shit-balls," Saki said as she scanned me from head to toe. "Are you ready for trick or treating?"

I stared at her.

"Duh, tomorrow is Halloween."

James and I nodded. Oh, right.

I peered down. I forgot I was in my Wonder Woman PJs.

"You also got something right here." Saki wrinkled her nose and pointed to her own hair to show me.

"Oh, it's just dried vomit." I pulled out a strand and examined it.

Saki and James reared their heads with crumpled faces.

"That's how my week's been going. Good way to start a Thursday, huh?" I groaned. "I'm gonna wait until they allow me to go back inside and get cleaned up. I'll go to the hospital. We'll talk later."

After everyone dispersed, I stood on the

lawn and stared at the smoldering wreckage. A wintry chill rushed through me. I couldn't shake the feeling that Max was behind the explosion or perhaps the hook man himself.

Ugh, the hook man. For a split second I'd erased him from my frontal lobe. But he was now on the top of my list of suspects.

A few more minutes passed, and they cleared me to return inside. As I spun on my heels and headed for the front door, my phone chirped. A text message from a trusted spy in my department, my old boss, Amy Puckett. My shenanigans at the bar had already made it to a desk in the Office of Internal Affairs.

That was fast. What else could go wrong?

CHAPTER 13

The next morning, I peered out my front window and savored my favorite morning beverage, a hot, chai latte, dirty. I'd hoped it was all a nightmare and I'd wake up to an intact vehicle. But it wasn't and my neighbor Gilbert Heart, the busy body, walked by with his dog and reminded me of that. Gilbert stopped, inspected the remnants of my crispy Highlander, and shook his head. When he saw me, he gave a hesitant smile, glanced away, and yanked his miniature poodle off her feet.

"Yep, that was me, I did that, almost blew up the 'hood." I nodded with my cup in hand and watched as he scurried down the block.

A few months ago, my neighbors hailed me a hero, until I returned from Florida. News traveled fast when a local parole agent with the Department of Corrections is involved in multiple shootings out of state. Although they cleared me of any wrongdoing, there's always that element of doubt.

As I let out a heavy sigh then sucked down the rest of my tea, I heard a knock at the door. Probably the squad ready to sit on my house again. But when I opened the door, a courier handed me a long, white box.

"Thanks." I nodded and peeked inside. Hmm, who would send me flowers? I set them on the dining room table and a note fell out.

It read: *G. Lil will contact you, xoxo, Teddy.*

The box contained four roses: one large red rose surrounded by smaller yellow, pink, and orange ones.

The peculiar flower arrangement was Teddy's fatherly way of letting me know he was around. The four flowers symbolized our family. Dear ol' Teddy was the red rose, and his gals represented the others. The last time he sent them, I was in a Florida hospital. As a matter of fact, he'd even sat by my bedside, but it didn't count because I was in a freaking coma. Heck, he bailed before I woke. The coward never stayed around. As usual.

"Screw this, he should be contacting me, not Grandma Lil." I walked over and pitched them in the trash. Just as I finished cursing him, my phone vibrated on the table.

"Unknown number? Maybe it's him after all." My heart pounded at the twinge of excitement.

"Hello, Rose?" A female voice said.

"Hi, Gran—"

"This is not a secure line," she replied in a sharp tone. "We need to talk ... in person. I understand you're heading out this way."

"I'm no—"

"When you arrive, you'll find a burner cell waiting for you with my number programmed. And bring the ... um bird," she said.

"Gran, I was thinking of not going."

"No, you must. You're in grave danger and I'm too old to be keeping any more secrets."

"Wha—"

With a crisp *click*, she disconnected the line.

I stared at the phone and shook my head. "What the heck? How does she know?" I plopped on the dining room chair in a daze.

Grandma Lil had always been cryptic, but this was eerie, even for her. I never grasped why someone who worked as a clerk for the State Department would be so paranoid. After she retired, she went off the grid. All I knew about her is that she moved to a secluded ranch outside of Darby, Montana.

"The bird?" I bit my lip and paced. "Oh, The Falcon. But what does Teddy have to do with it? What the hell."

I guess I was going to Montana. It'd be a welcome distraction from the hook man and my crispy vehicle.

CHAPTER 14

I woke late and quickly packed. As I set my suitcase by the front door, I caught a glimpse of my hair in the mirror. *Ugh.* I threw on my gold UC San Diego baseball cap and contemplated. "Saki's right, I look like Big Bird. Oh, well. It'll do the job."

In my haste I almost forgot my new black Columbia hooded jacket, so I put it on to make sure it fit over my thick sweatshirt. I read on the internet that you can wake up to fresh snow in Montana and be fishing in a T-shirt by noon, so layering's a must. As I shrugged one arm out of the jacket, the doorbell rang.

"I'll get it, Heidi." I looked at my watch. It couldn't be the Uber, it was eight o'clock, he'd said nine.

I opened the door. "Uh ... hello? What are

you doing here?" My mouth hung wide at Shilo.

"I apologize for not calling, but I left you a message. I heard about the explosion and was worried. All the news reports said a woman was taken to the hospital." She gave me a warm hug. "Are you okay?"

I pulled back. "Yesss." I stared at her eyes. They were so ... blue. It was like looking in a mirror. I could've sworn they were hazel before. I must be going crazy. I shook my head and removed my jacket and placed it on my suitcase.

"Um ... why are you here? Is it general practice for a house call? On a Saturday?" I stood with my fists on my hip. "Did my employer send you to check on me? Especially after ... you know." I rolled my eyes and fluttered my fingers in the air. "I kinda went off the deep end."

"No, nothing of the sort. I was concerned about you." She put her hand to her chest. "I thought we could chat."

"Ooo kay. Uh, but I've only got a little time." I motioned for her to come inside the entry.

"Oh, good, you're still going. Time away is an important step in the healing process. Especially now, you know, after your car exploded. I ... I'm pleased you're going," she said with a nervous laugh.

"Huh? Did I mention at our session I was traveling somewhere?" I held my arms tight to my body.

"N ... no, I ... I saw your suitcase and assumed you were planning a trip and I remember encouraging you to take time off, and … oh, I see you are taking a painting?"

I cocked my head.

She motioned to the large, corrugated box sitting by the door. "I assume that's what the box is for?" She scanned the living room and kitchen, then cleared her throat. "Uh … you know, I'm a bit thirsty. May I have a cup of tea and we can chat?"

I let out a heavy sigh, "Okay, the kitchen is this way." I gestured to the right. "I only have iced tea, is that—"

She disappeared from view and trudged around the front room, peering at the paintings on the wall. "You have beautiful taste in artwork. Do you have any others?" She wandered down the hall toward my bedroom.

I marched after her. "No. Uh, not at all. Unknown artists. I don't have time to chat or drink tea or talk about artwork. I've a plane to catch." I grabbed her elbow and re-directed her to the entry way. "Can we talk when I return?"

"Oh, sure."

I swung the door wide, and she dropped her car keys next to the empty painting box and bent down to retrieve them.

I intercepted and snatched the keys. The hair on the back of my neck stood.

She peeked inside, but why?

I ushered her out the door and escorted her to her vehicle.

A silver Porsche 911? Hmm, extravagant car for a shrink.

She slid behind the wheel and pressed the

start button. "Have fun in Montana!" She waved and sped away.

As I turned to the house, I paused. "Wait. Montana? I never told her where I was going. What the hell?" I snapped around to get her plate number. Crap, there was none.

I dashed inside and closed the door. My heart raced.

Heidi stood by the window peering out. "Rosie, who was that?"

I furrowed my brows. "She's the EAP psychologist my department sent me to the other day. But there's something odd about her." I brushed it off. "I've got one more thing to pack." I picked up the box and headed for the back of the house.

CHAPTER 15

A few short months ago, Titos sacked my house and wrecked my Lance Gun Safe, so I relocated my valuables. James recommended a safe room to secure my treasures: guns, silver coins, paperwork. Oh, and a five-million-dollar painting.

I entered my bedroom, then removed my wedding portrait off the wall, and set it on the bed. Today was the seven-month anniversary of Bradley's death. I rubbed my chest as tears formed behind my eyes. I shook my head. *Not now, Rose.*

I returned to the wall where I'd installed a control panel right behind the portrait. I hid a key in the panel, along with the code in the event I was incapacitated. Only two people knew about this, James and Saki.

The safe room was concealed at the back of my walk-in master closet. I sacrificed part of my wardrobe, but it was worth it. To the naked eye, it looked like any ordinary full-length mirror attached to the wall. But a closer look revealed a safe door.

Using the key, I opened the door and there it hung. The Falcon. I'd forgotten how magnificent it was.

"It's a shame, I may have to use the money from this to survive on if I'm unemployed." I let out a heavy sigh.

I handled the Falcon as if it were a newborn and wrapped it in bubble wrap and eased it into the corrugated box. I couldn't understand why Grandma wanted me to bring it, but she sounded adamant.

I stared at the box with my hands on my hips and it dawned on me that Shilo had searched for the Falcon. But why?

Suddenly, it was as if someone smacked me upside the head. I took a couple steps back.

"Oh my God, Shilo is working for Max."

CHAPTER 16

D r. Shilo Lane exited Rose's house and sped away, smirking as she passed the car's remaining charred debris. She parked at the corner, then pressed the off-hook switch on her Porsche. "Call, Maxwell," she demanded of the car.

"Yes," he barked.

Her body tingled at the sound of his voice.

"She's preparing to leave as we speak. I'll follow her to the airport."

"Perfect. Does she have the painting?"

"I believe so. I saw a paining box and tried peeking inside, but she caught me."

Silence fell on the line.

"Maxwell, are you still there?"

He drew a heavy breath. "It's Thomas and ... I need the truth from you."

"Of course, I ... I'd never lie to you." Shilo's heart palpitated.

"Did you have anything to do with her car bombing?" He asked slow and deliberate.

"What? How dare you. I am a professional and would not do such a horrible thing. I do not appreciate the accusation." Shilo huffed.

Admit nothing, deny everything was Shilo's motto. They trained her that way.

"All right, all right. But do I need to remind you that *no* harm comes to her. I couldn't care less about the rest of her people. But not Rose."

"Ma—uh ... Thomas. Your obsession with her is not healthy. It's time you move on with your life." Shilo pulled down the car's visor, revealing her lighted mirror. She removed lip gloss from her purse and dabbed it on with her ring finger. "You know, with someone more attainable. Someone worthy of your love." She put the gloss back and stared at her new blue sapphire colored contact lenses.

"Can't hear yo—on chop—see yo—Kalisp—" Thomas said.

"You're cutting out, Thomas."

The call ended.

"What I was saying." She stared in the mirror. "You need someone who will love you. Someone who will kill for you. Someone ... like me." Shilo flipped up the visor as she spotted Rose's Uber SUV arrive.

After forty minutes, Rose's ride pulled into the Auburn airport and she and the other woman unloaded their suitcases and ... yes, that big box.

Shilo waited until they departed then burned rubber out of the airport and sped down the Auburn Highway. She zipped into a shopping center and bolted inside the Suave Salon.

She darted up to a twenty-something year-old who stood behind the counter with her nose buried in her iPhone.

Shilo cleared her throat. "I called an hour ago about a cut and color." She spoke gasping for breath as she fumbled in her purse and removed her phone. She scrolled through it and found the picture of her latest client.

"I want my hair this shade of red, same cut too."

The gal ushered her to the back, where Shilo plunked on a swivel chair and dialed one final number.

"I'm delayed, so you have to do it. I'll send you a picture. You can't miss her, she's wearing a bright yellow baseball cap. Depending on the weather, she may also have a black knee-length coat. Hold on ..."

Shilo waited until her stylist went to mix the color. "You need to make sure it looks like a hunting accident. No witnesses. Make it clean."

She disconnected and smirked in the mirror.

CHAPTER 17

Once again, Kirk Tubberious, or as he asked me to call him, Uncle Tubbs, to the rescue. He was an old, trusted family friend and flew out from Miami on his Cessna Citation CJ4 to move his niece, Kaylee, back to Florida. Uncle Tubbs jumped at the chance to take a detour to Montana. Tubbs had friends there and was eager to do some fly-fishing.

As we made the hour and a half flight, a sense of déjà vu fell over me. The last time I sat in this plane, I was on a solo mission to Florida. But this time was different. No one was kidnapped, I'm not shot to shit, and I only brought one gun. I'd say it was a good start.

I half heard the conversation between Kaylee and Heidi and faked smiles and nods. It warmed my soul as Kaylee glowed with excitement at the prospect of bonding with her new sisters. Despite not being raised under the same roof and only meeting a few months ago, there was an immediate connection. She was family.

The more Kaylee chattered, the more she reminded me of Saki. Except her hair was strawberry blonde, long, and wavy.

As for Heidi, she chitchatted away and had a radiance about her too.

And then there was me. I looked at our trip as more business now than pleasure, a secret I kept from everyone. Ugh, I was so tired of the cloak-and-dagger routine. I felt like a covert operative.

My stomach flipped when we touched down in Montana. At last, long awaited questions were going to be answered about my cryptic family, especially Teddy.

It was noon, local time, when we arrived at the Ravalli County Airport. The landing was smooth and even. I thanked Uncle Tubbs for being a top-notch pilot.

He tipped his hat and grinned.

The second I stepped off the plane, I drew in the clean, crisp air. I closed my eyes, tipped my head back and stretched my arms, giving the sky a large hug. When I opened them, I peered up to the heavens and smiled, thanking God for making such a beautiful place.

It was sixty degrees, but in the direct sun, the temperature was closer to seventy. Not a cloud in the sky. Montana was aptly nicknamed

Big Sky with its wide open, endless views.

I stood speechless as I gazed at the Sapphire Mountains on one side, with the Bitterroots on the other. There was a light dusting of snow in the higher ranges. The view reminded me of Mom's famous chocolate cake with a fresh sprinkling of powdered sugar.

As Tubbs unloaded our luggage, he nodded to another pilot two planes over. When I turned to see who he acknowledged, the other pilot shied away and peered into his engine. He wore aviator glasses and a blue baseball cap, his brown flight jacket's collar was turned and hid his features.

My body trembled for a quick second and then stopped. Weird. Must be the change in elevation and the activation of my hunger button. I went to retrieve the Falcon, but Tubbs snatched it from me.

"Don't worry. I will take care of it," he said in his Greek accent. "Rosie, can you, ah grab me a soda from the pilot's lounge in the FBO, please? I'm parched. I will take your bags to the vehicle." He nodded to a white Escalade that just arrived.

"FBO?" Heidi asked.

"Ha ... sorry, Fixed-base Operator." He nodded to the building behind us.

I stared at him and back to the Falcon. "Okay, are you sure?" My voice shook.

He laughed. "Trust me, I know what it is." He winked and waved me onward.

CHAPTER 18

I entered the FBO's pilot lounge with Heidi and Kaylee in tow. It was a charming room with one receptionist, a brown leather sofa with matching love seat, and the smell of fresh coffee wafted in the air. I peered around the room and spotted the vending machine in the corner.

As I made my soda selection, a short, curly haired gal, about two inches shy of five foot and maybe one hundred pounds, bopped inside and approached me. Shuffling behind her was a six foot, roughly two-hundred-and-thirty-pounder with short, sandy blond hair. He looked more like a linebacker than a cowboy.

"Hey y'all." The short gal greeted me with a southern drawl and firm handshake. "You're Rose, right?"

"Yes, I am ... and who are you?" I drew my head back and wrinkled my brow.

"Oh, sorry. I'm Maggie, Maggie Banks, and this here is my baby brother Robert, but we call him Rebel. We're your humble guides." Maggie bowed and laughed. "I just love sayin' that shit." She elbowed Rebel in the stomach.

Rebel gripped his gut and let out an exaggerated "Oompf," snickered, and shook his head.

I greeted him and introduced them to Kaylee and Heidi.

Maggie had deep dimples with big hazel eyes and a nose piercing. She was a trampier version of Shirley Temple, dressed in cut-off denim shorts that barely covered her butt cheeks and a tight, low-cut, multi-colored western shirt. She wore brown and blue leather Ariat boots with a slight lift. Her outfit left nothing to the imagination. When Maggie turned away, I spotted a snake tattoo that ran the length of her thigh.

Rebel, on the other hand, did not say a word. He grinned like Gomer Pyle as he gazed at Kaylee with wide Labrador brown eyes. He wore Wrangler jeans and a long-sleeved denim shirt to match. His muddy Justin boots made it obvious he was a worker.

"There's a white Cadi for y'all out front, compliments of Mr. Marchetti," Maggie said. "Rebel and me are gonna shop for dinner. The cook is making elk stew for y'all. I programmed the address for the lodge in that fancy car. There's extra cars up there, so you don't need to go rentin' any."

"I don't know what to say. I'd like to thank Mr. Marchetti in person. Will we be meeting with him?"

"I ... uh ... not sure. Well, um, we gotta go. See y'all later." She waved and snatched Rebel by the shirt and bolted out the door.

Rebel turned and shot a wide grin at Kaylee.

"Someone has an admirer." I snickered to Kaylee.

"No, thanks, Sis. I just broke up with that cop from Key West. Not interested in anyone right now." She rolled her eyes.

Tubbs entered and advised us the SUV was all packed.

I handed him his soda.

"What's this?" He looked at it.

"Uh ... you said you were thirsty." My voice went up a note.

"Oh, so sorry. I forgot." He laughed and slapped the top of his hat.

Hmm, that was odd. I shook it off and exited the lobby.

On our way out of the airport parking lot, a classic pale blue Chevy pickup was parked in the dirt. A man with a black baseball cap was slumped down in the driver's seat, one leg hanging out the window, smoking and talking on his cell.

I stared as we drove by. Bradley would have dug that truck. He loved the classics. Except the way the guy was abusing it.

CHAPTER 19

Saki and James sat next to one another on handmade Amish cedar rocking chairs on the wrap-around porch, overlooking the Sapphires. They indulged in Napa Valley wine and hors d'oeuvres of grapes, imported cheeses, and crackers.

"They should be here any minute. Um, honey. Do you want to tell her Kevin brought a ... uh *guest?*" James asked.

"Nah, she'll soon find out. Besides, I don't think she'll care. Any spark between them was short-lived. Brad's only been gone seven months. Hell, she hasn't even really mourned him yet." Saki sipped her wine. She scrunched her nose and set it on the table.

"True, but Kevin has it bad for her," James said.

"Mmm hmm, but she—" Saki nodded to the lodge— "is his third, *friend*," she air quoted, "in three months. He's going through them like water. And haven't you noticed they all have a shade of red hair? And *this* one." She snapped her fingers. "Uh, what's her name. The tart, could be Rose's twin."

"Saki," James barked. "I've never known you to be snarky."

"Sorry, babe, my emotions have been wonky, maybe it's that time." She turned up her lip.

"It's okay, I like my women a bit jealous. Just don't poke her eyes out." He laughed and patted Saki's hand.

"I am not jealous. I wanted Rose and Kevin to hook up, and then he brings ... her." Saki jutted her chin and rolled her eyes.

James stood and pulled Saki to her feet. "Come here, wife." He planted a long, lingering kiss on her.

"Ugh ... you two, get a room." Kevin walked outside holding two hunting bows. He handed one to James. His latest gal followed.

"Are you two all settled?" Saki forced a smile. "Hey, Fanny, is it?"

"It's Fiona." She enunciated the *F* in her name, shrugged one shoulder, and shot a tight closed-mouth grin. "Fiona Uclid."

"Ha, F.U. are your initials?" Saki snorted.

"Like I have never heard that before," Fiona snapped.

Fiona's legs were to her ears and her long, auburn hair was layered. She let out a heavy sigh as she swished her way to the Amish table between the chairs and poured herself a glass of wine. As she bent over, Saki read LOVE scrawled across the back side of her pink and gray form-fitting yoga pants. Fiona wore a matching zipped up sweatshirt one size too small, with no under shirt, cleavage exposed, and flip flops.

"Are you wearing that hiking?" Saki raised her eyebrows and blinked.

"No, I just got out of the shower. I tried to convince someone to join me." Fiona giggled and patted Kevin's butt as she strutted past him, wine glass in hand.

"You know, Kevie. You said there's a spa here. I need a massage, and oh … a facial. It is so dry." She sighed again and touched her face.

Kevin put his fists on his hip and stood with one leg back. "No, Fiona, *outdoor* spa. Can you please go change for our hike?" He puffed his cheeks.

"Fine." She huffed, snatched the wine bottle, and stormed inside the lodge.

Saki cocked her head. "Kevin, what do you see in her? I mean, is she that good in the sack?" She widened her eyes and covered her mouth the minute it passed her lips.

James and Kevin snapped their heads in her direction. "Saki!" They spoke at the same time.

"Behave yourself. What's gotten into you?" James asked.

"Not sure, but you're right, I'm not myself. It must be the move … and Rose doesn't know."

"What. You haven't told her?" Kevin grabbed James's arm.

"I thought we'd get her liquored up and drop it on her. Speaking of, I need something else to drink, this wine does not agree with me." She pursed her lips. "I'm gonna find some soda or tea. You guys all good here?"

Kevin and James nodded as they peered through the sites of their archery bows.

"Boys and their toys." Saki chuckled.

CHAPTER 20

On our way to the lodge, I leaned my head back and closed my eyes. For the first time in weeks, my body melted, and I drifted.

It was raining and the homeless man stood across Shilo's office without his jacket. He used his hook arm and drew a line across his throat. But a saw replaced the hook and instead of cutting his throat, he sawed off his head. Blood shot out like a sprinkler and his head rolled on the ground. Just then a crocodile slithered up and bit off his leg. The hook man screamed, "Please, please help me. Don't leave me here." His facial features were distinct. "You. Did. This. To. Me. Rose." He spoke slow and deliberate.

"No, no. You're dead." I jolted and shot my

eyes open.

"Are you okay, Rose?" Kaylee patted my leg.

My breathing was labored, and I grabbed my chest. I blinked a couple times to refocus on my surroundings.

"You're so pale, like you've seen a ghost." Kaylee handed me a bottle of water.

"I think I did." I chugged the entire eight ounces. The last time I saw his face, he was human sashimi for a gator.

"You missed the cute shops on Main Street," Kaylee said as she peered out the window.

"Mmm hmm." I stared dead ahead as the hair on the back of my neck stood on end and goosebumps covered my body. The scenery was the last thing on my mind.

After a few miles, we took a left at a curve onto West Ridge Road and climbed three steep miles onto Hidden Creek. There were signs declaring *Private Property, No Trespassing,* and *No Hunting.*

The lodge, aptly named Hidden Creek Lodge, was not what I expected. It was more like a secluded mansion on a hill with its own private airstrip and unobstructed views of the Sapphire Mountains. It was the only house for miles.

His estate, as I preferred to call it, set on eight hundred heavily forested acres that dipped down into a private stream. The main house was 10,000 square-feet with six bedrooms and seven baths. There was an 1,800 square-foot cabin for the staff.

"This guy is uber wealthy," Kaylee said as we

pulled into a circular stone-paved driveway. "Holy moly, is that a wildlife themed fountain? And look ... a western saloon."

"Hey, I wonder if he's single?" I gave Kaylee a nudge and a wink.

"If only." She laughed.

Kaylee and I were first to pop out of the SUV. The second my foot hit the driveway, a chill ran down my spine. I felt my forehead with the back of my hand. Hmm, no fever.

Kaylee handed me my bag and coat and made her way inside with Heidi, while I stood with an open mouth and gazed at the two-story log mansion, with its timber pillars. Man, who was this guy? He was rich as ... Max. I shuddered at the name.

I turned to get the Falcon, but Tubbs pushed past me.

"No, no, no. I will take it to your vehicle." He patted my arms.

"Okay." I peeked around him into the rear compartment.

"Tubbs, why is the box different?" I pushed him aside.

"Oh ... um." He rubbed the back of his neck. "I changed boxes after we landed." He gestured with his hands. "See." He opened it. "It's all good, my Rosie." He cupped my face. "Don't worry your pretty little head."

It was rare I let anyone talk down to me. But with Tubbs, it was different. I knew it was heartfelt and not condescending. So, I'd let it pass, just this once.

I tilted my head and pursed my lips. "Is

everything okay?"

He put his hand to his heart. "I promise, Rosie, unblemished. Now go pick out your car." He jutted his chin to the stable of vehicles that were backed in a neat row.

"I'll take that one." I pointed to the silver Chevy Tahoe, as I stared at Tubbs.

I never noticed how thick his accent was when he was nervous.

But why was he nervous?

CHAPTER 21

After my wary interaction with Tubbs, I approached the guys who stood on the deck inspecting their hunting bows. They looked like a couple of kids playing with their new Christmas toys.

"Well, hello, Red." Kevin gave me a warm hug and stepped back. "You were laid up in a hospital bed the last time I saw you. You look much better today," he said with a twinkle in his eye.

"It's Rose, not Red, thank you." I shot him a closed-mouth grin.

James once told me Kevin only gave nicknames to people he liked. But I was not in the mood.

James greeted me with a warm embrace and whispered, "I had doubts you'd make it."

Just as he loosened his bear hug, a twenty-something, bluish green-eyed filly bopped out. She met my height, but I had a few pounds on her. If I were ten years younger and wore my boobs as earrings, we could've been twins.

So that's what Kevin was into? Hmm. Never figured him as a ta ta man. I smirked.

"Is this better, Kevie?" She strutted in front of us and modeled her form fitting fleece-lined hiking pants and even tighter matching low-cut sweatshirt.

"Oh, hi, I'm Fiona." She spun around. "You must be Rose. I've heard so much about you." She hugged me as if I were a long-lost sorority sister.

"Hi?" I flashed James and Kevin a quizzical peek over her shoulder and pulled away. The hugging was over the top. "I've heard nothing about you." I cleared my throat and exchanged glances between the guys.

"I'm from Miami Beach and I'm a swimsuit model. Hoping to make the cover of Sports Illustrated next month. I just graduated from Florida State University. I was head cheerleader." She tossed her hair and looked at her reflection in the lodge window.

Jeezo, when I told her I knew nothing about her, I wasn't expecting her resume. I nodded and put a finger to my lip. *Keep quiet, Rose.*

"Thank God you're here, Rosie," Saki said from behind the screen door as she bounced out and gave me a hug. "Aww sis, our alma matter." She pointed to my bright yellow baseball cap. "Oh, here's a package for you."

She handed me what I assumed was the burner phone.

They all furrowed their brows at me.

"It's from Grandma Lil. I'm headed to her place," I said.

"Oh? We were all going for a hike. Please, join us," Kevin said with dilated pupils. His sea-green eyes disappeared with his smile.

"I ... I have stuff to do." I cleared my throat.

James gave me a sideways look. "You just got here, how can you have anything to do? You're supposed to relax, remember." He put his pinky in the air.

"Yes, please." Saki shot me her puppy eyes. "You'll miss out on getting acquainted with Kevin's new girlie of the month," Saki said, tipping her head from side to side.

I wrinkled my forehead and squinted. Her behavior was peculiar and very catty.

Kaylee came out dressed for the occasion and introduced herself to Fiona. They were closer in age, with undoubtedly more in common.

"We're burning day light," Kevin chimed. "And we don't want a cat fight breaking out." He looked at James and turned back to Fiona. "It's getting cold, you should wear a jacket and hat."

"Uh ... noooo," Fiona sang. "I just spent a bundle to get my hair done. I'm not wearing a stupid hat, it'll get messy. And I thought we were going out tonight, you know, dining and clubbing." She flashed a toothy smile.

"Haaa, is that the lie you told her, Kevin?

There's no clubbin' here, sweet cheeks." Saki snorted. "And I promise to help you with your hair if it gets messy. You wouldn't want a bird shitting on you, would you?"

"Saki!" I scolded.

"Not tonight, honey." Kevin turned to Fiona. "The chef is making elk stew and homemade corn bread. Plus, James and I are hunting tomorrow, and have to be up early." He pulled her closer to him. "And you gals are going on a guided fishing excursion tomorrow."

"Excuse me? I am not fishing. I just got my nails done. I thought we were yachting," Fiona whined.

"I explained the trip to you, no yacht, just rafting down the river. Look at this place, it's awesome." Kevin waved to the outdoors.

"I wasn't really listening. Besides, I don't have a stupid hat or a coat. And I am not wearing my fur on a hike." She sniffled.

"Here, Fiona." I handed her my jacket and hat. "Use mine. I promise they're clean."

"Thanks." She shot a snarky smile and stomped away. She paraded in front of the entryway elk mirror with different poses and duck lips.

"O.M.G., Kevin, where do you get them from, Bimbos R Us?" Saki stood with her fists on her hips.

"Saki," I snapped again.

"What? It's the truth." She shrugged with her palms up in the air.

"Saki. Come with me for a second. I have something to give you," I said with wide eyes as

I pulled her to my Tahoe. "What the hell is wrong with you? Be nice to Kevin's girl uh— friend or whatever." I flailed my hand.

"You mean, piece of ass." She mocked.

"See? I've never known you to be snarky even when you're on your period."

"I'm not." Saki looked the other way.

"Then what?" I said.

She sighed. "I don't know ... my hormones are wonky, and I feel fat ... and that should be you with Kevin." She nodded to the lodge and pursed her lips, "Not bimbo Barbie."

"Oh my God, I can't believe I did not see this. You're pregnant." I put my hand over my mouth.

"No. I took a test. Well, a few. They were all negative. It's just that I'm eating more and the stress of us moo—" She let out a puff of air and glanced back to James.

"Wha? Huh? You guys are moving? Did you buy a house? Is it in my neighborhood?"

My voice went up an octave.

"Um ... a little farther away." She scrunched her nose and pulled her shoulders to her ears.

"Where?" I crossed my arms.

"James!" She yelled and looked back to him.

CHAPTER 22

"**W**hat is it honey?" James hurried to us.

"Rose knows. I'm sorry." She lowered her head.

James pulled Saki closer to him and put his arm around her. He placed his hand on mine.

"Rose, we wanted to tell you in California, but with all that happened, we just couldn't," James said in a low, soft voice with a tilted head.

"Where the hell are you moving? Can you tell me *that*?" I yanked my hand from under his, crossed my arms, and stared, tongue in cheek.

"I got a position on the SWAT team. But it's in Miami."

"Oh, okay. Well, congratulations. Thanks for

telling me, I uh … am ecstatic for you both." I looked away. The words barely passed my lips and my bottom chin trembled. An intense pain seared my heart as if someone shot a dagger through me. They were both leaving me.

I cleared my throat and let out an enormous sigh and opened the vehicle's door. "I need to go. Grandma Lil is waiting."

James closed it and turned to Saki. "Hey babe, can you give us a minute? Try on that new battery-operated warming jacket I bought you. With the matching gloves."

Saki hugged me and whispered, "I love you. I'm so sorry." Tears fell down her rosy cheeks.

I wiped them. "I love you more. It's okay." I forced a smile.

"I'm sorry too, partner. I meant to tell you the day you laid me out in the alley. But you wer—"

"It's Rose," I barked as I stared past him.

"Huh?" He pulled his head back.

I returned my gaze to him. "James, everything is changing so fast. We're no longer partners. I'm not Red," I snapped and nodded in Kevin's direction. "I may not even be Agent O'Brien anymore. I'm just Rose. Hell, maybe I'll return to the Reagan name." I opened the door again and slid behind the wheel and swallowed hard. "Anyway … any word on the investigation?"

"Good job, don't deal with your problems and change the topic," he snipped. "And, no, Jon will call me with any new leads." He slammed my car door.

I flinched and stared ahead.

"Oh, I figured out who's been following me." Yes, I was the queen of avoidance.

"Who?"

"I saw his face in my dreams." I put my head on the steering wheel. "It's Titos. The hook man is Titos. And I know Max sent him, but don't know why." I gazed at James.

"What?!" He marched in circles with his hands on his head and shot back to me. "Are you freaking kidding me? He is dead. I was there, remember? There were no signs of life in the swamps ... and plenty of blood." James crossed his arms and stood with a wide stance. "You are chasing a ghost, Titos is gone. I thought coming here would be good for you." He gestured to the lodge. "You need to relax. Felicity, please, come hiking with us." He softened his voice again and shot me his buck eyes.

"James, Titos is alive. I can feel it. I'm rarely wrong about these things. My dreams can be very prophetic." I choked back a sob.

"You know how crazy you sound? You need help. Why don't you call that shrink ..." He snapped his fingers. "What's her name?"

"Shilo?" I barked.

"Yeah, her," he replied.

"Are you freaking kidding me! She's in on it, too." I furrowed my brows.

"That's enough." He pounded his fists on the hood of my car. "You have to stop this, right now. Once again, you're avoiding the real issue. Get out of here." He tapped my head. "And work on healing." James put his hand over his heart. "You're edgy, angry, and paranoid. And you have not smiled in God knows how long."

"I wish you still believed in me." I pressed the button and started the Tahoe.

"Felicity, I love you like a sister, which you kinda are now." He gave me a light shoulder punch. "I'm not leaving you. I am here and will always be. Whether we are in the same state, or not."

James looked back as Saki yelled the gang was ready. "You gonna be okay?"

"I'm fine. Go." I turned and tears rolled down my face. I could not let him see me cry. I peered in the rearview mirror and watched James walk away with his head low. *The AP to my Felicity.* And now I'd never hear that again or see his silly Austin Powers routine. The thought was too much to bear.

I closed my eyes. It occurred to me, he was deserting me, just like all the other men in my life.

I wiped my face with my sleeve. "Suck it up, Rose."

When I removed the burner cell from its package and powered it on, there was an awaiting text message from Grandma. She instructed me to meet someone named Lily, at the last gas station in Darby at a quarter to two.

I put the Tahoe in drive and left. On my way out, the same old blue Chevy pickup that was parked outside the airport drove past me. The same guy sat behind the wheel with a cigarette hanging out of his mouth. As we passed, we made eye contact. He looked like a tweaker and my guess is that he'd smoked more than cigarettes today. I peered above his head and spotted a hunting rifle secured in a rack behind him.

Hmm, where was he going? There were no other houses up there and hunting was prohibited on the property.

My scalp tingled.

CHAPTER 23

It took ten minutes to get to Main Street. On the drive up the hill, I'd missed the brilliant shades of reds and yellows. Fall was a season that was short-lived or non-existent in California. As I rolled down my window and drew in the fresh, clean air, a chill ran through me. My hooded sweatshirt didn't cut it, and I instantly kicked myself for lending my jacket to Fiona.

When I parked the Tahoe, my stomach grumbled. The time on the dashboard read one. I missed out on lunch, so I set off to find food. As I passed by a card shop, Halloween decorations were being replaced with turkeys and gourds. An overlooked holiday nowadays.

My delight turned somber as I looked at the forlorn face staring back at me. My hair stood up like a cockatoo. I forgot I loaned Fiona my hat too. I pulled my hair up into a high ponytail, but the new 'do did nothing to help the miserable looking woman in the window's reflection.

James was right. I hadn't smiled in months. Because I didn't have a reason to. The holidays would be dismal this year, with Bradley gone and our mother dying just after Christmas last year. Now Saki and James were leaving.

I gulped back tears. Wow, Saki's hormones weren't the only ones out of whack.

My stomach growled again, and I spied pastries displayed in the next window. The Montana Rose Beanery. A smile almost formed at the name. I walked inside and ordered my favorite chocolate croissant, and hot tea, any flavor as long as it was caffeinated.

As I waited for my beverage, I inhaled the chocolate bliss and gazed at the passersby. They smiled and made eye contact at one another. What a concept. I felt as if I'd stepped into a Hallmark movie and the town opened its arms to embrace me.

All of a sudden, the sweet Hallmark film turned into a horror flick. I stared and could not blink. An electric shock surged from head to toe. There he was, gimping along on the opposite side of the street. But he was clean shaven, and his hair was trimmed.

What the hell? Why? How? Where did he come from? I'd had a feeling he'd be here, somehow.

My legs went weak and hands tremored. As I

stood frozen, I didn't hear my name called. The barista approached and touched my shoulder. I jumped and flailed my arm, spilling hot tea on the floor.

"I am so sorry, ma'am ... I'll make you another." She used her towel and wiped up my mess.

Everyone stopped their conversations and stared as if I were an alien who just invaded the town.

"That's okay." I raised my hand to her and bolted out the door. I peered left and then right, but he'd vanished. I hustled to my Tahoe and slipped behind the wheel. My hands shook as I fumbled to find my cell. I found it lying at the bottom of my bag and called James.

What was I doing? He wouldn't believe me. After three rings, I ended the call.

I pressed the button to start the vehicle and sped off to the only person who would get me, Grandma Lil.

Ghost, my ass, Titos is alive!

CHAPTER 24

"I am sorry for my behavior, Fiona. I'm not myself." Saki turned to the other woman and apologized.

Fiona cocked her head and returned a wry grin. She trailed behind everyone, cursing, as she tiptoed over branches like a ballerina.

"I guess I feel guilty about abandoning Rose," Saki confessed to the group.

"Oh, we all are, Saki," Kaylee chimed in as she ducked under a branch. "After we leave Montana, we're headed to Florida. Rose is going to help me get settled. That can't be easy for her."

"Oh dear. I thought about returning to Florida as well, but perhaps I should stay with Rosie a little while longer. She is so hard to read and is closed off, like her father," Heidi said.

Silence fell in the air at the mention of his name. "Well, I wouldn't know. Don't remember him. He split when I was two." Saki's face reddened. "Although, my entire family lied to me and said he died in combat."

"Well, Sis. At least you weren't conceived in prison, like me." Kaylee linked her arms into Saki's.

Saki let out a huge snort laugh. "Ha. That's right, good old Teddy hooked up with your mom in federal pen. She was a nurse, right?"

"Yeah, she fell in love with him. I've never met him." Kaylee shrugged.

Saki removed one glove and grabbed Kaylee's hand. "We have each other." She unzipped her coat and turned off the battery. "Hey babe, this warming jacket works wonders. I'm hot as hel—" Saki put her hand over her mouth. "Heck. My apologies, Heidi."

"Oh please, after living with Maxwell all those years and his cronies, a little *hell* word won't offend me." Heidi chuckled.

"Hey, speaking of chums ... what ever became of D.O.G?" Saki asked.

"I'm not certain. Douglas and Lucy are probably somewhere on a tropical island." Heidi scoffed.

"Well, they can rot for all I care. They about blew me up in the boatshed." Saki shook her head.

"Oh, forget all of them. This is such a lovely hike, and the leaves on this tree are a deep red. It's absolutely glorious." Heidi stopped.

"Listen." She put her hand to her ear. "The water is flowing pretty darn fast. I love that sou—"

Out of nowhere a doe popped in front of them, her fawn hopping close to her tail.

"Aww." The ladies said in unison as they cocked their heads.

Fiona didn't stop. She mumbled something inaudible under her breath.

"Hmm, something must have startled them," James said. "I think we're getting kinda deep in the forest. Time to head back."

"Thank goodness!" Fiona huffed and was the first to high tail it. She bolted and tripped over a branch. Just as she went down to her knees, a shot whizzed past the group and hit a pine tree, inches from where she fell.

"What the hell!" Kevin rushed to Fiona. "You okay, sweetie?" He helped her to her feet.

"Does it look like I'm okay? Someone fired at me … and I'm not your sweetie." She yanked her arm away and removed pine needles from her clothing.

James ran to them. "Uh, Kev. It's still archery season, right?"

"I thought so. That's why I brought mine," Kevin said.

Kevin and James removed their pistols from their holsters, their heads on a swivel. Kevin looked one way, James the other.

"Hey. There are people over here, asshole," Kevin shouted into the trees. He looked at Heidi. "Sorry ma'am."

"It's fine. I'm certain I saw signs that said no

hunting when we pulled into the lodge," Heidi replied.

"Are we still on the owner's property?" Kaylee asked.

"Yes, we are." James scurried back to Saki and held her close to his side.

Fiona whispered something in Kevin's ear and jogged ahead of the group, dodging branches.

Kevin looked to James, threw his palms out and shook his head.

As soon as Fiona hit the clearing near the lodge, two more shots rang out in her direction, nicking Rose's jacket.

"Drop to the ground, Fiona!" Kevin yelled. "Everyone drop. James, can you get a visual on the shooter?"

James and Kevin took cover by a tree trunk. While everyone but Fiona ducked. She sprinted to the lodge.

"Hey fuckhead, there's no hunting allowed on this property," James shouted.

"Sorry, dudes. My bad," a male voice called out.

Kaylee and Heidi bolted up and followed Fiona's lead.

Saki stayed by James's side.

"I think this asshole was shooting at Fiona. It was no mistake." James sighed and shook his head.

"What are you thinking?" Kevin asked.

"Does she have any enemies?" James inquired.

"Fiona? Nah." Kevin shook his head.

"Isn't it peculiar that Fiona is wearing Rose's jacket and baseball cap? And they kinda look alike." Saki ducked down next to James, her heart pounded like a Taiko drum.

James stopped and stood quietly for a second. "Nah ... it's obvious this doofus can't shoot worth shit and was poaching."

James helped Saki to her feet.

"Yeah, probably right. Oh, by the way, we will have one less guest for dinner. Ms. Fiona is packing and headed to Missoula. She's staying the night in a hotel before she takes off tomorrow. She is done with me and *nature shit*." Kevin air quoted.

"It's my fault, isn't it?" Saki lowered her head.

"No. I knew it was a mistake to bring her. I don't know what I was thinking. I am not that into *her*."

Saki watched as Kevin raised his brows to James.

Maybe there's hope for Kevin and Rose. Saki smiled as her body tingled.

CHAPTER 25

The drive to Darby was a quick jaunt South from Hamilton. En route, I kept peering in the rearview mirror looking for suspicious vehicles. "Stay alert, stay vigilant," I muttered.

Instead of enjoying the scenic drive through the valley, a heaviness developed in my chest. Something was wrong. My instincts were on target, most of the time. I picked up the phone to call Saki and have her cancel the fishing trip tomorrow, but then I remembered how excited she and Kaylee were about going.

"Nah, that would be too selfish. Besides, they all think I'm unhinged." I shook my head as I pulled into the town of Darby.

Less than three minutes and I arrived at the last gas station. Darby was an old timber and mining hub, charming and picturesque. But I was in no mood to play tourist again. A couple minutes after my arrival, a motorcycle approached from the south side. The pipes roared and could be heard for miles in the valley, even with my windows closed.

As the bike came into town, it slowed to the posted speed limit of twenty-five. The driver turned her head in my direction. I couldn't make out her features because the helmet's face shield was blacked out. All I could see was an American Flag decal on the back.

The rider's long black hair was in a single, tight braid and she wore blue jeans and western boots of sorts. She had on a black leather jacket with matching gloves. She drove past me and turned around two blocks away at a local bar.

As I looked back, I removed my 9 mm from my concealed carry purse. Everyone was questionable to me. It was an occupational hazard.

I held my gun by my side and assessed my wardrobe. I wore my navy-blue alma mater sweatshirt with the Trident mascot on the front, Miss Me blue jeans, minus the bling on the ass, Justin boots, purple, mirrored Maui Jim aviators. Oh, and the icing was my high ponytail. Yeah, I was intimidating. Not. I didn't think I'd need any ass kicking clothing on my holiday.

The gal pulled up next to me, shut off her bike and removed her helmet. "You Rose?" She jutted her chin.

"Who's asking?" I replied as I clicked off the safety from my gun.

"I'm Lily Cazier. Your grandma sent me." Her hazel eyes narrowed.

"Oh, hi, Lily." I let out a puff of air and turned off the Tahoe. "Sorry for the inquisition. I don't trust many people." I put the safety back on and stuffed it in my shoulder bag.

"That's something we have in common." She snickered.

"Hey, cool chopper," I said as an ice breaker.

"Thanks, it's a 'sixty-six Genny Shovelhead. It was my father's. Now she's mine. We don't have many good riding days left. Um, hey." She looked behind us. "You sure you weren't followed?"

"No, I was watching."

"Okay." She jumped off her bike and pulled out a retractable long handled mirror from her saddle bag. I recognized it and used a similar one on my job.

I popped out of the Tahoe and followed her as she made her way, searching the undercarriage. Lily stopped at the rear driver's side and shook her head. She dropped to her knees and removed what appeared to be a tracking device.

The veins in my neck protruded. "What the h—"

She put her hand to her lips and waved me away from the vehicle.

"What the hell?" I said in a hushed voice. "I don't understand why the owner of the lodge would do this."

"He or she obviously does not trust guests with their vehicles." She chuckled. "But maybe your Grandma can run a check on the owner. Do you have a name?" Lily asked.

"I think Thomas Marchetti. I was going to leave a thank you note before we left. Humph." I shook my head.

"Oh, one more thing, turn off your cell. It can still be tracked, but unless the NSA is after you, that's unlikely. We'll run a debugging device through the vehicle too."

I shot her a puzzled look.

Lily put on her helmet, returned to the Genny, and nodded for me to follow.

"Paranoia my ass," I muttered.

CHAPTER 26

"It's all set up, Mr. M." Maggie spoke into the car's speaker phone as she and Rebel pulled up to the lodge. "Me and Gav are gonna take all four ladies fishing tomorrow. We will have a boat waiting up there. While Rebel and Joe take the guys huntin'."

"I don't know and don't care who these people are, just do it. But keep me posted. And do I need to remind you that no harm comes to Rose. Under any circumstances," Thomas demanded.

Maggie motioned for Rebel to take the groceries into the lodge and turned off the Bluetooth. "Yeah, yeah, I got it. Um, whatcha want done with the other three, Kaylee, Saki, and that hot model? I know a guy who might be interested. They are the shit, and we can get a pretty penny for 'em."

"I don't care. Money is of no consequence to me. Do what you want with them, but don't tell me. All I want is Rose, unharmed. Also, I want that painting she brought with her. I will be sending someone for it," Thomas said.

"Huh? Don't know about no painting. Rebel and me went shopping when they got here. I think they are all out on a nature hike or some shit like that. I'll search their rooms and get back to you."

"You need to find that painting!" Thomas ordered.

"Okay, okay. When y'all getting here?"

"We are about halfway. We will be landing at six this evening, local time. I'll be at my lake house. I have a business meeting."

"All right. Um, how about the old lady? She was not part of the plan."

"Oh, Heidi, the traitor? No harm to her, either. I doubt she will want to go fishing. She will probably stay behind and knit or read. But keep her occupied. Have someone take her t—"

Shots rang out.

"Hey, boss, I gotta go. I think some asshole is poaching on your property, again. Rebel and me got this." She disconnected the call and saw what she assumed was Rose, running from the rear of the property into the house, followed by Kaylee and Heidi.

Maggie grabbed a rifle from the gun rack and rushed toward James and Kevin.

"What the hell happened?" she asked.

"An asshole. Hey, let me ask you. It's still archery season, right?" James asked.

"Yeah, no rifle yet. I'll bet it was a fuckin' poacher," Maggie snapped.

"I'm not so sure. He fired three shots in Fiona's direction. Almost hitting her."

"That ain't cool. Rebel and me are gonna find that mother. We've had assholes up here poaching."

"Yeah." Kevin scratched his head. "Maybe we should call the sheriff's department. I'm a personal friend of Sher—"

"No! No cops," Maggie blurted. "This here issue will be handled the local way."

Just then, an old faded blue truck zoomed down the hill, kicking up dirt and rocks.

"That must be him. Let's get him," James said.

"Nah. I know who he is, a local tweak. Rebel and me got this." Maggie winked.

"I don't hear anything." Kevin covered his ears and looked at James. "Oh, and by the way. You're going to have one less guest. Fiona is packing and on the first flight back to Miami."

Maggie waited until Kevin and James entered the lodge. She groaned and took her phone from her pocket and texted: *Wat the fuk u doin up here Gav?*

CHAPTER 27

After trailing Lily a few miles, we turned right onto West Fort Road. We continued ascending for another fifteen windy minutes and took another sharp right onto a rocky, dirt road. A wooden handmade sign hidden from view read *Lone Coyote Lane.* "How fitting," I mumbled.

Grandma's entrance was another mile from the main highway and lined with pines and firs. I had the feeling I had eyes on me and then spotted a camouflaged camera. Okay, so I wasn't being paranoid.

We pulled up to a seven-foot black Fortress Ornamental Gate with wood pickets. The fencing around the front was more of the same. Both practical and eye-fetching.

Lily nodded to what I assumed was another

concealed camera. The gates opened inward, and we drove ahead. Once inside, two dogs greeted us. One was a Staffordshire Pit Bull Terrier, and the other was a gargantuan of a breed I didn't recognize.

They growled and bared their teeth at Lily, but she appeared unfazed. She popped off her bike and removed her helmet. They immediately tackled and greeted her with wet kisses.

Grandma waited on the front steps, laughing at her pups. Her eyes crinkled in the corners when she smiled. The last time I saw her, her hair was still blonde, now it was silver. Her face was more relaxed than in recent years. Retirement looked good on her. If it were not for the neck brace and cane, she'd look sixty-five, not seventy-five.

The second I opened my SUV's door, the dogs turned their attention to me. They approached with their hackles high. My heart raced. I was a dog lover, but these two made me want to check my underwear. I stood still as they sniffed me. Then it was game on. They wagged their tails and drenched me with their slobber.

Phew, chonies still clean.

"They are harmless until they're not." Lily peered around me. "The pit is Stevo, and the Cain Corso is Brian."

"Oh, I've never heard of a Cain Corso," I said.

"It's an Italian breed of mastiff. They are used for protection, tracking, or companion. In

Brian's case, he's all three. And a big cuddle bug too. They are trained killers, but pussycats with the right people. I can tell they like you. You passed the test." Lily laughed.

"Uh, I'd hate to see if I didn't." I stood and dried my face with my sweatshirt sleeve.

"I knew you would." She patted my arm.

"Sitz," Grandma said. The dogs sat at attention and waited for another command with perked ears. "My motto is you can fool some people some of the time, but you can't fool a dog. They know who to trust." Grandma limped toward me.

Stevo kept wagging his tail and smiling as he sat. His whole hind quarters did a jig. Gotta love Pitties.

My eyebrows furrowed as I pointed to her cervical collar. "You did a number on yourself."

"Yeah, I don't do anything half-ass. But maybe I should try." She laughed. "At my age, being thrown from a horse is not what it used to be."

"So that's the story?" I snickered.

"It's a mild sprain and twisted ankle. But all that matters is my tiki tiki boom boom is still working." She patted her heart. "And you can sit and complain, but it doesn't do any good. You gotta push, scream, and sometimes cry. But I don't cry." She scrunched her nose.

"That is Saki's nose," I said.

"Come on, let's go to the back deck. You can see everything from there. Oh, I assume you brought it?" She peered around me and looked at my vehicle.

I nodded back to her.

CHAPTER 28

We circled around to the back of the house and I stood with my mouth agape. The views of Trapper Peak were breathtaking. Grandma's backyard was fenced with an acre of luscious green grass just for the dogs. They even had their own agility course.

The wrap-around deck overlooked a private two-hundred-acre horse ranch, two ponds, one loaded with trout, Grandma said, pointing. Three sides of the property were walled with the same material as the front entrance. The rear backed to thousands of National Forest acres.

"The guest log cabin matches the main house on the outside." Grandma eased onto her cedar bench. "It's close to three thousand square feet and has two master suites on opposite sides of the house, a laundry room, and fireplace."

Lily came out with a couple of glasses of red wine for Grandma and me. "Griz and I share it," she said.

"Griz?" I pulled my head back.

"Yeah. His name is Tom Grizwald, but we call him Griz. He spends most of his time in that stall barn." Lily motioned to a building almost the size of my house. "It has fifteen stalls, a wrangler's shed, and tack room. He's another of Lil's rescues. I think her favorite." She shot Grandma a closed smile.

"Rescue?" I squinted.

"Your Grandma loves broken people. And horses." Lily snickered.

"Ah." I nodded. "Where is he?"

"Buying supplies in Missoula today." Grandma stood and motioned for us to go inside the house.

"Here it is." She opened her arms as if saying ta-da. "It took me years to get it the way I want it. Thank God for smart investments." Grandma winked.

I gazed up at the vaulted ceilings with enormous windows.

"It is thirty-nine hundred square feet. It's got four bedrooms, three and a half baths, granite kitchen, massive master suite, office, laundry, wine room, and double attached garage," Lily said.

"Sheesh, you sold me. You could be a real estate agent." I wandered around the living room and peeked through the dual sided fireplace.

Lily grimaced. "No, thanks. Too peoply. And you have to be nice all the time." She poured herself a glass of cabernet.

"I get it." I took a sip.

"But you know, at my age, it is too much to handle, and since I am rescuing more Mustangs, I've hired on two other ranch hands. They are in the background process," Grandma said.

"Background?" I asked.

"Mmm hmm, I'll explain later." She sat on the couch and took a sip of her wine.

Just then a plane flew low and landed in the back.

"You have an airstrip too?"

"Yes. And Tubbs just arrived."

"Ah, so *you* are the friend he was talking about, I should've known." I snuffled. "His Cessna can land back there?" I peered out the window.

"No, he's using my plane. He's running an errand for a friend and won't be staying. Now ... I think it's time we have that chat, Rosie."

"Yes, we do. Gran. I need your help. Someone's been following me."

CHAPTER 29

After I brought Grandma up to speed on my life, including Titos' ascent from the grave, she insisted I stay for dinner. She had a pot roast in her slow cooker, and I salivated at her invitation.

I turned on my cell to call Saki and received a voice message from James.

"Gran, someone shot at Fiona. Maybe a poacher? She's returning to Miami. But I tell you, he said something intriguing. She was the only one shot at and coincidently was wearing my coat and hat. Not to mention from a distance she could be my doppelganger." I gulped the rest of the wine.

"Okay, after dinner, we're going downstairs," Grandma said.

Griz came home two hours after I arrived and joined us for dinner. He was a sketchy character and stood about five foot, eleven. He had shoulder length black wavy hair, with a closely trimmed beard and mustache. If I were to guess his age, I'd say close to Lily's, somewhere in the mid-twenties.

He was a man skimpy on words and mostly nodded and grunted. But his smile was genuine, there was a good feel to him. He kept his past close to his vest, and I did not interrogate. There was enough on my plate.

But, like Lily, Griz worked for Grandma and asked no questions. I figured she saved him from a certain hell, and he owed her. And if she trusted him, I did too.

After our brief meet and greet, he removed his coat and gloves, and I was immediately drawn to his hands. He was sleeved in tattoos from knuckles to his shoulder. I'd seen my share of prison tats, but these were done on the streets. But the most fascinating of his body art were the numbers 3-7-77, tattooed on his left shoulder.

During dinner I wanted to ask him about the digits, but my gaze was fixed on a control panel attached to the wall next to the door leading downstairs.

"That was amazing roast." I stood and helped Griz and Lily clear the table.

"Ready, Granddaughter?"

"I was born ready."

She walked over to the panel and flipped open a metal compartment and placed her face up to the machine. Lights flickered and scanned her eyes, unlocking the door.

"What is th—"

"Biometric Iris Scanner," Grandma said.

I blinked a few times and stared. "I'm impressed."

"You haven't seen anything yet," Lily said as she and Griz made their way downstairs.

Lily was right. I stood at the bottom of the steps without saying a word. It was the size of her main floor, but on steroids, minus the kitchen. At first glance it looked like your average guest quarters complete with a soft brown leather sofa sleeper, two matching recliners, coffee table, dining table, powder room, oh, and four, seventy-five-inch-high-definition smart TVs.

The televisions took up the entire north side of the wall. A long L-shaped modular workstation covered the south side. I walked around and gawked at her toys.

"Holy cow, you have your own communications center." I perused her electronics. "This is James Bond accoutrements."

I nicknamed it her war room. She'd equipped it with one desktop computer, three laptops, a Ham radio and a land line telephone. Grandma had five closed circuit television monitors for all of her surveillance cameras that surrounded her property.

"I don't need to remind you to keep it on the down low. All my staff sign a waiver of secrecy when they work for me. I have them all vetted too," Grandma said in an offhand manner.

"Grandma, um … what did you do for the CIA?" I looked sideways.

"We'll talk about that later. First, let's run your guy. What's his name?" She sat down on an executive leather office chair at her desk and placed her right index onto a USB fingerprint scanner.

Another Biometric security device? I shook my head. "Uh, his name is Tony L. Titianos, he was in the FBI and assigned to the Miami-Dade Office." I stood behind her and crossed my arms. "I still can't believe he survived the croc attack. There was so much … blood." I shuddered as I recalled the snapping of his arm and the screams.

"Hmm … according to the records, he's dead. Here is his death certificate." She looked at me.

"Grandma, I assure you he's not. Somehow Max put him back together, like freakin' Humpty Dumpty," I said as if I were pleading my case in court.

"Okay. I believe you, honey." She patted my hand. "Let's see, there are a few hotels in town." She clicked away.

"Gran, how do you have access to all this … stuff?" I waved my arm around her room.

"Don't ask a question you don't want the answer to," she replied.

"So, that's where Teddy got that saying from, ha."

"Yep … here we go. An Anthony Tito is registered at the Valley Inn. It's at the north edge of town. There's a bar right across the parking lot. Looks like he paid in cash. We can snatch him either tonight or tomorrow. Your choice." She swiveled her chair around and faced me.

"Uh ... snatch?" I slowly said as my gaze met hers.

"You know, bring him back here and interrogate him," Grandma said matter of factly.

"He's a big dude, and not cooperative. An asshole, like his boss." I snuffled.

She stared at me and just blinked her eyes, pursing her lips.

"Okay, don't ask a question I don't want the answer to." I tipped my head to every other word.

"We'll get a key to his room and grab him. You mentioned earlier he's a drinker?" Grandma asked.

I nodded.

"I'll bet he's in the bar," Grandma said.

Griz and Lily sat quietly during the entire time, watching a previously recorded Montana Grizzlies football game on one screen. Stevo and Brian were curled up on the bear rug, belly up, snoring.

"I'm on it." Lily grabbed her phone and traipsed upstairs.

A few minutes later, she yelled down. "He's there. The bartender said there was an obnoxious man with a hook. He's been there every night till closing. I asked her to keep him there. It's almost nine o'clock, they close at eleven. I better hurry." Lily walked out the front door.

"Can she?" I asked.

"If it's that brunette with the great rack." Grandma put her hands to her breasts. "She can do it."

I stood with my mouth opened and shook my head. "Grandma!"

"Hey, she has to use what God gave her." She shrugged.

"So, we grab him and bring him back here. Hmm." I rubbed my chin. "We should do it tomorrow. I need to return to the lodge and check in with everyone."

"Sounds good," Grandma replied as we went back upstairs and finished cleaning.

"Okay. So ... how do we get the key? You know, I can always go to the front desk and tell them I locked myself out," I said.

"Or ..." Grandma peered behind me.

I stood silent and stared at Lily. She wore a tiny black mini skirt with teal and black studded cowboy boots. Her hair was down to her rear. She was 5'4" but her legs made her look 5'9".

"Yeah. That's better." I nodded.

"Hey, you're hot stuff, don't burn yourself," Grandma blurted.

"Lillian." I laughed out loud for the first time in months. "I think that's where Saki gets her unfiltered profane tongue."

I turned back to Lily. "You look beautiful, by the way."

She curtsied and giggled. Lily opened the

hall closet and pulled out a brown suede coat.

"Here, that sweatshirt won't cut the evening chill." She handed it to me.

"Thanks. Now that my new coat has a bullet hole through it." I rolled my eyes.

"Okay." Grandma interrupted us. "You grab his key, and we'll chat with him tomorrow."

"I should be there. He is unpredictable and dangerous," I said.

"No. He'll recognize you. We got it handled." Lily grinned as Griz emerged from downstairs, with the dogs in tow.

"That works. I'll trail you guys out, so I don't get lost." I turned and hugged Grandma. "We never had that chat," I whispered.

"Later. We need to find out what Titos is up to first." Grandma pushed me out the door.

CHAPTER 30

Titos sat at the Valley Bar, or as the locals called it, the VB. It was two-hundred feet from his hotel room and attached to the restaurant with the same name. The VB was a popular, intimate hangout for tourists and locals alike. The bar had low intensity track lighting, sports on every channel, and 'eighties music at a moderate level in the background. Animal mounts covered the walls, and a fireplace was lit for ambiance.

Since he was the only one left at the bar, the bartender gave him all her attention. After his fourth Montana Honey Whiskey, he was ready for another. He pulled his cell from his jacket pocket and texted his accomplice: *Let me know when you arrive.*

He set the phone on the bar and stared at his

hook. Soon he'd be able to afford a new hand. He threw back another shot.

"Maybe I'll get a bionic arm. Chicks dig that. What do you think?" He slurred at the voluptuous brunette pouring him another round. "Should I get a bionic arm and leg? Hell, I'll get a bionic pecker too. Shit, I'll be the six-million-dollar fuckin' man."

As he downed his drink, she strode into the bar. She was the most beautiful creature he'd ever seen. She wore a short black miniskirt and cowboy boots. Her silky black hair fell to her waist. Her round hazel eyes made his groin flutter.

She stared at him and glided to the bar. "A shot of the same, please," she said.

"Put it on my tab." He almost fell off the stool as he gawked at her legs.

She smiled with ruby red lips. "Thank you." She raised her glass and took a shot. "Another please and I'll take it over there." She motioned to the corner.

He grinned and followed her with his eyes as she sashayed, sliding into the booth.

He ordered a bottle and limped over to her. "May I join you?"

"Perhaps," she said in a seductive voice.

"What's your name?"

"Lily. And yours?"

"Tony, but my friends call me Titos." He grabbed her hand and kissed it. He excused himself and went to the bathroom.

After a half bottle of the VB's finest whiskey, Titos gave the farm away. He told Lily he was going to come into a lot of money and could whisk her off to any tropical island of her choosing.

He lied about his injuries and said he was blown up during one of his secret operations with the FBI. But he assured her his manhood was still fully intact.

He grabbed Lily's hand to show her.

She yanked it back. "Not so fast. Later." She winked at him.

"This whiskey is getting to me. You sure you didn't slip me a mickey or sumtin?" He slurred again.

"I would never do such a thing." Lily's voice trembled as she laughed.

"Hey, don't go nowhere, I gotta take a whiz, again." Titos slid out of the booth and weaved to the bathroom.

A few minutes later he returned to the table. A mysterious looking man with tattoos over his hands and knuckles was sitting with his date.

"Who da fuck are you?" Titos asked.

"Oh ... um, he's my brother, Griz," Lily said.

"Oh, good. I thought you was stealin' my gal. I'd have to fuck you up." His east coast accent was stronger the more alcohol he consumed.

Griz didn't reply. He cracked his head and knuckles and downed his beer.

"Okay, sexy, it's time to go," Lily said.

"Hey, I don't do guys. It's just us two, right?" Titos wobbled his head back.

"Of course. My brother's leaving and I'm gonna rock your world. Um ... where is your room key?"

The earth rotated as Lily and Griz assisted Titos the few hundred steps to his hotel. The second he entered the room, his vision narrowed.

CHAPTER 31

I woke at 5:45 in the morning and couldn't get back to sleep. The guys left for hunting and the gals were still sleeping, so I crept out of the lodge. There wasn't much open this early on a Sunday, so I went to a drive-through and ordered my usual chai. As I sat waiting, it occurred to me today was a Holy Day. I was to refrain from engaging in work or anything that hinders reverence to God. Instead of going to church, I was committing a sin. Not sure what commandment I was breaking, but a few, no doubt.

I sat at the end of Main street and waited for Lily and Griz. They pulled up at seven o'clock sharp. Lily jumped in my ride as Griz drove ahead in a white Ford Cargo Van, with no rear windows.

On our way to Titos's hotel room, Lily and I discovered we had more in common. She told me her parents were killed two years ago in a plane crash.

"So how do you deal with it?" I asked.

"I don't. I keep busy and your Grandma helps." She grinned.

"I get that. I'm so tired of people telling me I need closure." I rolled my eyes.

"Closure is overrated," she replied.

"That's what I say." My voice went up a note.

"I've been told that I'm angry and need therapy." Lily snarked.

"Ugh, me too." The hair on the back of my neck stood on end. It was like I was listening to myself.

"So, what is Griz's story?" Yes, I was the queen of changing topics to avoid talking about painful things.

"What do you mean?" Lily cocked her head.

"You said he was a rescue too, like yourself. Where does he come from?" I asked.

"All I know is he's a native Montanan, as was his family. He keeps his past closed, and I don't ask. It's his story to tell," Lily said.

"I totally get it." I nodded. "He has a lot of tattoos, but one piqued my curiosity. What do the numbers 3-7-77 stand for? I've seen it on the patches of the Montana Highway Patrol. Was his father a trooper?" I asked.

"He doesn't talk about it. The numbers are a true Montanan mystery. The troopers wear it to honor the first people in Montana who served to protect the citizens. One theory is it stands for Montana Vigilante. The original vigilantes were Masons and swore an oath of secrecy. The last one took it to his grave. But one thing is certain, if someone found these numbers tacked on their cabins or tents, they better leave town, or else," Lily said.

"Humph, maybe Griz is the silent, but deadly type." I chuckled.

"Nah, he's only deadly to those who do his loved one's harm. Other than that, he's a real softy." Lily removed her seatbelt.

"Well, here we are. Just back in next to Griz," she said.

As I exited the Tahoe, I froze. It occurred to me what we were doing was illegal and not to mention a bit evil. But a necessary evil, I assured myself.

Lily must have sensed my apprehension and grabbed my arm. "Are you sure you're ready for this? There's no going back."

A lump developed in my throat and I tried to swallow. I looked at her. "Let's do it."

My job was to stand guard and be the eyes and ears of our covert operation. I kept my head on a swivel.

As Griz backed up the van, Lily used Titos's card key and propped open the rear entrance. The two had it down to a science, so it was most likely not their first time.

I didn't ask.

When Griz came to a stop, he peeked his head out and I gave him the thumbs up. All was clear. He popped open the rear double doors from the inside and yanked out a gurney and ushered it inside the hallway.

Lily went to the passenger side of the van and grabbed a cup of coffee from the cup holder and retrieved a vial from her pocket. She jutted her chin and I nodded in response. Lily poured the contents of the vial into the coffee and bolted inside the hotel.

Titos's room was on the first floor and the second one to the right.

Griz and I stayed outside with our ears plastered against the door.

Lily propped the door open with the latch in the event things did not go as planned.

It was 7:20, and Titos was still sleeping when Lily entered. "Good morning, Handsome," Lily said, loud enough for us to hear.

I rolled my eyes at Griz and put my finger in my mouth in a gagging motion.

He grinned.

"You rocked my world last night," Lily said in a seductive tone.

"Huh? Oh yeah, the hot chick from last night." Titos sounded groggy.

"I bought you a coffee. Ready for round two?"

"You know, I don't remember doin' you last night." Titos slurped his java.

"Oh, but you did." Lily giggled like a schoolgirl.

Titos bought it hook, line, and naughty girl.

A few moments later, we heard a loud *thunk*.

That was our cue.

Griz zoomed the gurney inside and lowered

the stretcher. I closed the door and the three of us grunted and groaned as we loaded Sleeping Ugly. Titos was ginormous and weighed an easy two hundred and fifty pounds. As Griz strapped him in, I peeked my head out the door to make sure the hallway was clear.

We bolted out as quick as the stretcher allowed and heaved him into the van.

Lily and I jumped in my vehicle and followed Griz.

"He is out like a light. What did you give him?" I inquired.

"A little Special K." Lily winked.

"Perfect! Pay back is a bitch. Max gave that crap to Saki when he kidnapped her." I grunted. "Did you give him enough? He's a big boy."

"Yep, a little more than a full dose. He's still out of it from last night," Lily said.

"So, now what's the plan?" I asked.

Lily peered over her sunglasses. "The rest is up to Lil." She wore a cheeky grin.

As I drove back to Grandma's, a sudden rush shuddered through my body. It was my first abduction, and it was ... exhilarating.

CHAPTER 32

Saki woke with a wave of nausea. She hustled to the bathroom, but nothing came out. "Hmm, no fever." She felt her forehead as she splashed water on her face. "Must've been the elk stew. Not eating that again." She pulled her lower lids down and peered at her eyes and pale skin in the mirror.

A light rap interrupted her private conversation.

"Wake up sleepy head, it's seven o'clock. Time to get moving." Kaylee opened the door and bounced into the bathroom. "Hey, are you okay?"

"Hi." Saki said weakly as she bent over the sink. "How's your stomach?"

"Great, why?"

"The elk stew did not agree with me." Saki

pursed her lips.

"Oh?" Kaylee touched Saki's forehead and face. "Hmm, no fever. I have antacid in my room. I'll get it."

"No thanks, Doctor Sis." Saki faked a smile. "I have some. Let me get dressed."

Kaylee closed the door.

Saki opened her overnight bag, popped a couple antacids, and got dressed. She looked around the room for her new jacket and found it on the antique fainting couch with a note from James. She smiled as she read it:

I love you, wife. I know you will miss me, so until I return, this should carry you through the day. Since I can't wear it hunting, I sprayed it on the paper.

PS. It was a gift from the lodge owner. Take a whiff.

Saki waved it under her nose and immediately dropped it. "What the fuck!" she yelled. She felt her face turn white and her stomach tightened. She read the bottle. *Made in Italy. No.* The last time she smelled that wretched scent, she was in the presence of a maniac.

She tried calling James, but it went straight to voicemail, so she left a frantic message.

Saki bolted down the hall to Rose's room, hoping she was still there, but she'd left. She called Rose's cell. "Crap. Isn't anyone answering?" she shouted at the phone.

Saki flew downstairs, screaming for Kaylee, but she was waiting by the car.

She ping-ponged from room-to-room

downstairs and called out for Heidi.

Just then Maggie flung the door wide. "Let's go, Princess," she barked.

"Where is Heidi?" Saki shouted.

"She ain't joining us today." Maggie grabbed a paper sack off the kitchen table. "Here." She tossed it to Saki. "Since you overslept, the cook packed you a brown bag breakfast."

Saki caught it. "Not hungry, thanks." She stuffed it in her jacket pocket and snatched Maggie by her shoulders. "Who the hell owns this lodge?" she bellowed.

Maggie reared her head back and stared at Saki's grip. "Do not ever do that again." She threw Saki back a couple feet. "Don't like being touched. The last person who did that ended up in the hospital." Maggie shrugged.

"Sorry, but you have to tell me, where does the owner live?" Saki snapped.

"I don't know, Italy or France." Maggie pushed her out the door. "Come on, Gav is waiting. And he don't like to wait. Hey, where the hell is Rose? It's like herding fuckin' cats with you guys." She peered back at the house.

"She's not joining us either, she's spending the day with our grandmother," Kaylee replied as she scrolled through her phone.

"What the hell, you kidding me?" Maggie growled. "This was not part of the plan," she muttered, almost under her breath.

"What plan? What are you talking about?" Saki shot Maggie a quizzical look.

"Uh, not plan ... trip. I meant trip. Now get your ass in the car." Maggie opened the door and pushed Saki into the backseat.

Kaylee zipped to the other side and jumped in next to her sister.

On the way through Darby, Saki's nausea worsened, and her hands grew clammy. She continued to interrogate Maggie about the owner but didn't get an answer. Maggie exchanged several silent glances with Gav.

Saki spoke to Kaylee in the backseat in a hushed tone as she told her the after shave was one-of-a-kind designed for Max.

"You know Sak, the owner is from Italy. Maybe it's sold there?" Kaylee patted Saki's hand.

Saki pulled away, sat back and crossed her arms. She didn't buy it. If Rose taught her anything, it was to trust her instincts.

"Something's not right. Stay on your toes," Saki whispered in Kaylee's ear.

Kaylee's eyes widened, and she nodded.

Something's wrong. Chills ran down Saki's spine.

Her suspicions would soon be confirmed.

CHAPTER 33

Lily, Griz, and I pulled up to Grandma's lair at about eight o'clock. The gates opened, and we made our way through. She stood outside and waved us to the backside of her house, toward the walk-out basement. It was a separate room attached to the house with a fortified door.

Grandma opened it and there was another room approximately twelve by eighteen square feet, with concrete floors and no exterior windows. It was a cross between a prison cell and an interrogation room. The only furnishing was a fixed metal table with two matching chairs.

Griz wheeled Titos out from the van and secured him to the gurney with three leather straps. The kind used in psychiatric facilities to confine the violently mentally ill.

Since Titos was missing his left leg from just below his knee and left arm from the elbow, restraining his prosthetics posed a challenge. I stared at this damaged, unconscious man and flashed to the crocodile attack. I shuddered again and almost took pity on Titos, but quickly dismissed it.

Griz locked the gurney's wheels in place, and we walked through the room and came out the other side. The second door was the entrance to Grandma's command center/war room.

Grandma drew back the curtain to reveal a one-way, mirrored glass. Bullet proof, I assumed.

"I didn't see this last night." I furrowed my brows as I stared at Titos from behind the window.

"It was on a need to know," Lily said.

"You passed the test. And now you know." Griz followed.

"You mean by drugging and kidnapping? Is this passing the test?" The second the words passed my lips, the reality of it all smacked me upside the head. I'd just committed a felony. Holy crap. If anyone found out, I could lose my job. Worse yet, I could go to prison. I worked in those places. I couldn't go to prison. Bile surged in my esophagus and I bolted to the downstairs powder room.

Grandma hobbled after me.

"What did I just do, Grandma?" I splashed water on my face and stared at her in the mirror.

"I told you it was going to be a bit unconventional." She rubbed my back. "You'll be fine."

"I know, I know. I guess I wasn't ready for ..." I waved my arms in the air. "This! Whatever this is ..." I nodded to Titos' cell. "And what do you use that room for?"

"We occasionally get unwanted guests and need to have a conversation as to the nature of their visit. No one comes on my property without a proper invite and screening." Grandma walked out of the bathroom.

"Conversation? Now I am afraid to know." I shook my head and followed.

"Excellent choice." She smirked.

"Grandma. You were not a clerk for the State Department, were you?" I stood with my hands on my hips.

"Let's have that talk." She grabbed my hand.

"What about him?" I pointed to Titos.

He rolled his head, mumbled a few words, and dozed off again.

"He'll be knocked out for a while. Don't worry, Lily and Griz will make sure he doesn't choke on his own saliva."

I stared at him in silence.

CHAPTER 34

A t eleven o'clock Sunday morning, Dale drove Thomas, a.k.a., Maxwell Ryan, to the airport in Kalispell where a business associate, Chena Fin, flew in from Canada. Moments after a Customs and Border Protection Agent exited Chena's private Stream, she made her way down the steps toward Thomas's Cadillac Escalade Limo.

Chena had only been a voice on the other end of a telephone during art auctions and Thomas didn't have a clue as to what she looked like. But she had a shark's reputation and was the best and most discreet art advisor. She was an attorney by trade and represented the most ruthless in the art business.

But why were they meeting in person? It was not industry practice to make face-to-face art deals. The high-end art world was all about secrecy. The buyer and seller never met, nor were their identities revealed. Thomas grew more suspicious of their meeting. Did his buyer back out of the deal? If so, why didn't she just call?

The instant she sauntered closer, Thomas was in awe of her striking beauty. While he preferred red, her long black silky hair with streaks of silver shimmered in the brilliant sun. She wore a black pantsuit and boots with a red London Fog jacket and black leather gloves.

Thomas rolled down the tinted rear passenger window.

Chena peered over her Gucci sunglasses. "Mr. Ryan?" she asked.

"It's Marchetti now." He pursed his lips. "Miss Fin, I presume?"

Dale was out of the driver's seat in an instant and opened the rear door of the SUV limo.

Chena slid in across from Thomas. She removed her gloves and neatly folded them, placing them on her lap and laid her sunglasses on top.

Thomas sat silently for a minute and studied her features. Chena was in her mid-forties and an Alaska Native American with deep, dark brown eyes.

She cleared her throat. "I see you made it through Customs last night. Did you raise any suspicions?" she asked stoned faced, all business.

Thomas shook his head. "Uh ... no problems. I switched the documents. My paintings should not be on anyone's radar. Besides, I don't think customs agents are trained to tell the difference between a Rembrandt and a Monet." He smirked and raised his brows.

"Perfect."

"Chena, may I call you that?"

She nodded.

"Why are we meeting in person?" Thomas crossed his arms.

She jutted her chin to Dale. "Your driver needs to go."

"Dale, take a hike." Thomas turned his head and ordered.

Dale looked back to Thomas. "It's cold out there and I don't have a jacket."

"That is not a request. Get out, now." Thomas ordered. "I'm finished with him after this trip." He let out an exaggerated sigh and returned his attention to Chena.

"We have a problem that you need to resolve."

"Excuse me? Are you telling *me* what to do?" Thomas's admiration for her dwindled. "I don't work for you or anyone else."

"Maxwell, we all work for somebody."

"My name is Thomas!" he barked.

"I know all about you. You're a wanted man. You avoid sanctions and you like to clean your money through your shell companies. And if you don't want the feds kno—"

"That's enough. I get the picture ... what do you want?" He glared.

"It's not what I want. It's what you have to do for all involved."

"All?"

"You, me, my boss, and other alarmingly powerful people I can't name."

"Look. You tell your boss, if he requests my assistance, he needs to reach out to me personally. And like I said, no one orders me around. Take that to him." Thomas wore a smug grin.

"That's not going to happen. You see, to relay such information could be detrimental to your health. My boss has more connections than the president. And ..." She drew a heavy sigh and looked to her lap. "He doesn't know I'm here."

"Who do you work for? You know, since we're breaking all the secrecy rules," Thomas asked.

"I can't tell you. And it is not my job to know the identity of my bosses. I'm an intermediary. I advise and do not question. I just do ... and it's bigger than him." Chena's voice trembled.

"Just tell me," Thomas snapped.

"All I can say is that someone released confidential buyer and seller information."

"So, what do I have to do with it?" He shrugged. "My legal name is not on any document."

"You don't understand. *Max*! The anonymity has been stripped away from many influential people, my boss included. And *you* are going to find the source."

"Why me?"

"There is a mole in the art circle, and he is feeding incriminating information to the feds."

"How do you know the spy is a male? And how is *he* doing that?" Thomas sat back and crossed his arms again.

"A reliable source informed me a man only known as the Ghost is using one of your paintings to relay the information. The way the Ghost is doing it is unknown. And personally, I don't care. All I want is him and the painting terminated."

"I have a stable of paintings. Which one?" He raised his brows.

"The Falcon."

"Are you crazy? I'm not going to destroy the Falcon. Besides, I don't have possession of it at the moment."

"He is not using the real Falcon. There is a copy. And you're going to get it," Chena said.

"I will see what I can do. I'll get back to you." He looked out the window.

Chena let out an exaggerated sigh. "You don't seem to understand. I'm not making a request either." She glared at him as she slipped on one glove and then the other in a slow, deliberate manner. "You have twenty-four hours. I will be in touch." Chena exited and returned to her plane.

Thomas sat and stared at the empty seat in front of him.

For the first time in his adult life, he'd met his match.

CHAPTER 35

"We're done for today. The fish ain't bitin'," Maggie said.

"That's fine with me." Saki set down the fishing pole. She felt queasy the entire morning and kept thinking about the cologne. But one thing was certain, the beauty of Montana was captivating. For a moment she stopped ruminating and peered at the peaks, closed her eyes, and drew in a deep breath.

"Don't let it fool you, these mountains can be deceptive," Gav said with an evil intent in his voice as he snuck up behind her.

Saki jumped and opened her eyes. There was something creepy about Gav.

"Gav, shut your mouth, you don't know what you're talking about." Maggie punched his arm.

"Well, you all live in such a wondrous place.

When did you and your brother move here, Maggie?" Kaylee asked.

"Uh ... Rebel and me ain't been here that long. Less than a year. We moved from Texas."

"Yeah, I noticed your accents," Kaylee said.

"Enough chattin', it's 1:30, y'all hungry?" Maggie asked.

"I'm starved." Kaylee patted her stomach.

Saki and Kaylee stepped out of the fishing raft as Maggie and Gav pulled it to shore.

"I know a little place, but we gotta climb a bit." Maggie nodded up the hillside.

"Yeah, the views are to die for." Gav snickered.

"You are a moron." Maggie hit Gav in the back with a paddle. "Sorry about him, he ain't right in the head," she said.

"I'm game. How about you, Saki?" Kaylee asked.

"That's fine. A hike would be good for me." Saki stared at her fishing guides.

Maggie handed out the brown bag lunches and bottled water.

Fifteen minutes later and up a gradual incline, they were at the top of the mountain.

Saki and Kaylee stood side by side with their arms wrapped around each other. Kaylee took out her cell and snapped a selfie of them and sent it to Rose.

"Look at this view. It's amazing. This is God's country," Kaylee said with a wide smile.

"Phew. I'm getting warm. The sun is baking me." Saki removed her warming jacket.

"That's funny. I was just getting cold. I didn't

pack a thick enough coat."

"Ha, that's right, Ms. Florida. You're not accustomed to any cool weather. Here, let's switch." Saki handed Kaylee her jacket. "The warming gloves are in the pocket, but you probably won't need them."

"Hey, I have to use the bathroom." Kaylee peered around and did a jig.

"I have one better. It's the perfect location. And we can have lunch there, too." Maggie waved them over, with Gav in tow.

Saki's suspicion of Gav grew. Maggie was correct, he wasn't right in the head. He reminded her of someone who did too much meth. People her sister warned her to stay away from.

Gav kept peering over his shoulder.

"What are you looking for?" Kaylee asked.

"I'm on bear security," he replied.

"Bears!" Saki and Kaylee said at the same time as they shot a look to one another.

"Don't worry. They are uh ... in hibernation," Maggie said as she slugged Gav in the arm, again. "Don't scare them, dumbass."

He rubbed his shoulder and glared at Maggie.

Saki watched as Maggie shot daggers back at him. If looks could kill, Gav would be dead.

"We're close. It's right over that little hill. There's also a picnic bench and a stream, that's where we'll eat." Maggie tramped ahead of the group.

A few moments later, they came upon a grass-covered mound. And as Maggie said, there was a bench, but it was smashed to pieces.

"Uh ... sorry ladies, a bear must've destroyed it." Gav laughed. "You can pee over there. It's on the other side." He pointed.

"Perfect," Kaylee blurted, as she made a bee line.

"Hey, I'll go with and, you know, stand guard." Maggie followed.

Saki nodded and opened her bag and took a bite of her turkey sandwich. She put it back, her appetite gone. She went flush again and ambled over to a steady running stream and splashed cool water on her face. Her thoughts kept going back to the cologne and Max.

Ten minutes passed and Saki peeked at her watch. She was lost in thought but noticed that Gav disappeared too.

Just then Maggie emerged from behind the knoll, without her sister.

"Where's Kaylee?" Saki cocked her head.

"Uh ... she is going number two." Maggie smirked and held up two fingers like a child.

"Oookay. Where is Gav?"

"Ah, he is probably out doin' what guys do out here." Maggie peeked in her bag, pulled out a sandwich and wolfed down the whole thing.

"The running water is giving me the urge too." As Saki stood, pain seared through her chest.

Something was wrong.

CHAPTER 36

Maggie led Saki to the outdoor "toilet."
One side was a grassy knoll, the other was the entrance to a dark underground room obscured by fallen tree branches.

"What is that?" Saki asked as she peeked inside.

"It's an abandoned root cellar." Gav emerged from the room.

"Put your hands up, Princess."

Saki spun on her heels. Her heart skipped a beat as Maggie stood there with a gun in her hand.

"What the fuck are you doing? And where is my sister?" she said through gritted teeth.

"You'll see, now move." Maggie nodded to the cellar. "Gav, take her cell too."

Gav removed it from Saki's back pocket and tossed it to Maggie.

Maggie snatched it and smashed it beneath her boot. "We don't want no one trackin' you. I know they can. I seen them movies. Now get inside with your sister." She shoved Saki.

As Saki tripped into the cellar, she spotted Kaylee lying on the ground, not moving. A battery-operated lantern illuminated her sister's face. She ran over and shook her. Kaylee didn't respond, but she was breathing. Her ankles were bound by steel leg shackles and she was handcuffed to a metal pipe that was attached to a concrete wall.

Saki bolted to her feet. "You bitch. You're gonna pay for this." Her neck felt red and hot with tension as she expelled angry billows of air.

"Ha, fat chance, Princess." Maggie sneered.

"Are you going to kill us?" Saki growled.

"Nah, if I were gonna do that, I would have done it in the river," she replied.

"Hee, you know it's legal to bury a body in Montana." Gav snickered, picking at his face.

"What's so funny, you tweak?" Saki stepped inward toward Gav, rotated her foot, and hips, adding force to her jab. Her mixed martial arts training kicked in.

Gav wasn't ready and was thrown backwards, hitting the wall. He sprung back and swung for Saki, Maggie grabbed his arm in mid swing.

"Stop. I don't want her face bruised," she yelled and glanced around the room. "Gav, where are the other restraints?"

"I couldn't find any more, so I got these." He pulled zip ties and handcuffs from his jacket pocket and twirled them from his fingers.

"Well, fuck me running with a hayfork. You *are* an absolute moron." Maggie shook her head and let out an exaggerated sigh. "Just give her the shit, will you?"

Saki launched at Maggie, reaching for her weapon, grasping, but she was too late.

Gav grabbed her and covered her mouth. Saki felt that familiar poke to her neck and slapped his hand. It worked quicker this time. Her legs went weak, and she slumped into Gav's arms.

He exhaled a loud "Oof" as he caught Saki, but she slipped from his grasp and slid the rest of the way.

Gav restrained her arms first and then legs.

She couldn't move but heard and saw everything. "Fu ... you." She slurred as the world around her blurred. She swiveled her head to the left and saw Kaylee's face. Before her vision completely telescoped, the piercing sound of a gunshot rang out.

Saki's body recoiled.

CHAPTER 37

Ⓘt's a bummer y'all didn't get anything."
Rebel tossed the hunting gear in the back of
Joe's Chevy pickup and slammed the
tailgate.

"Come on, dude. We gotta go." Joe sat in the
driver's seat and gestured at Rebel.

"It's okay, we had a great time." James
watched as they kicked up rocks and ripped out
of the dirt parking lot. "Wow." James coughed
and waved the dust away from his face. "What
the hell is their hurry? I was gonna invite them
for a beer at the brewery in Darby." He jumped
in the passenger seat of the Denali. "You game,
Kev?"

"Heck yeah, partner." Kevin shot a thumbs
up as he started the GMC.

It was close to two o'clock when the guys

departed the trail head off MT- 43. As they made the mile drive to Highway 93, James turned on his cell phone.

"Holy cow. I've got three voicemail messages. All marked urgent." James puffed his cheeks. "Oh, boy. Now Saki's on a tear about Max. Something about the aftershave the owner left us." He rolled his eyes and played the next message. "Hmm. I'm an ass." He furrowed his brows and turned to Kevin.

"I could've told you that." He jabbed James in the shoulder and chuckled.

"No, I'm serious, dude. Someone drugged Rose."

"What?" Kevin pulled his head back.

"Yeah, my buddy who works for the Department of Corrections said a local patron at the bar where Rose went after her shrink appoin—"

"What? Shrink?" Kevin asked.

"Long story, I'll fill you in later. But this guy felt bad for her and came forward. He witnessed the whole thing. Rose walked in and ordered a coffee, like she said. After a few minutes, she went to the bathroom. Another man with a hook came in behind her and paid off the bartender to put gamma-hydroxybutyric acid in her coffee." James ran his hands through his hair.

"What the hell! Why would this *hook* man give Rose GHB? That's a date rape drug." Kevin pounded the steering wheel.

"That's not all. The bartender then started giving Rose shots of booze. That's why she sounded drunk ... because she was. *Crap.* I'm sorry I didn't believe my partner." He sighed and shook his head.

"Hey, it's okay. She'll forgive you. Is that why she's in hot water with her supervisor?"

James bit his lip and snorted. "No. During her drunken stupor, she phoned her boss and called him a *pencil dick-twat waffle.*" James air quoted.

Kevin laughed. "Gotta love that Red."

"What? Love?" James snapped a look at Kevin.

"Like ... I meant, like. Not love. Pfft, I don't even know her. Anyway. What else? You said you got three messages."

"Oh ... my buddy Jon, the lead in Rose's car explosion, said it was not an accident. A bomb was wired into the vehicle's security system. It was activated when Heidi remotely unlocked the doors. He said one of her neighbors' cameras captured a Porsche 911. The driver pulled up at 2 a.m., got out and rolled under Rose's Highlander. The suspect wore all black and a ski mask."

"So, Rose is right, someone's after her." Kevin pressed the accelerator. "Crap, this truck is a slug up hill. Once we get over the pass, it's all downhill, buddy." Kevin leaned forward in his seat as if that would speed up the Denali.

"I've got a bad feeling, Kev. This free trip, the bombing, her coffee being spiked." James scrolled through his contacts and called his favorite IT gal. He put her on speaker. "Hey Daisy. I need you to run a records check on a

Thomas Marchetti. I don't have a DOB, but he's from Italy. If that helps."

"You got it, Boss." Daisy spoke as if she were a hamster on a wheel, her nails hitting the keyboard at lightning speed.

"I'm losing cell reception and need to make another call. Can you text me the info? Oh, I need this stat. Thanks, Kiddo," James said.

"Copy that." Daisy disconnected the call.

James dialed one more number. "Ugh, straight to voicemail. Rose is probably still pissed at me. I don't blame her."

James left a detailed voice message of his findings.

"Finally, over the pass." Kevin smiled. "We should get there soo—" He pumped the brakes. "Shit. I can't slow down!"

The GMC fishtailed on the icy pavement. It swerved left, then right, and left again, smashing against the guardrail. All four wheels left the ground and careened off the side of the mountain at fifty-five miles per hour. The front end contacted a small tree and they flipped.

Kevin shouted something, but James's heart pounding muffled the sound. *Thump-thump, thump-thump.* His inner organs twisted like a pretzel as a vision of Saki with a baby bump flashed before him.

The vehicle was airborne for what felt like an eternity, until, for a split second they made contact again with another tree and then flipped vertically and then horizontally. James lost count how many times they overturned.

The world spun slowly in front of him. Their

flasks, backpacks, satellite and cell phones flung around the cabin. As they bounced ferociously down the snowy mountainside, the sound of crunching metal magnified in James's brain.

Out of his peripheral vision, debris from the SUV fell off, piece by piece as the vehicle hit one branch after another. Trees hammered all four tires and the frame. The smashing abruptly stopped. There was no movement.

Dead silence.

The Denali landed at the bottom of the canyon, upside down.

James slowly looked over to Kevin as beads of bright red blood plopped onto the steering wheel.

What happened to the airbags?

CHAPTER 38

"**W**ere you an analyst or ..." I looked around the room, leaned in and murmured, "*secret agent?*"

"You don't have to whisper in my house, I sweep it all the time for bugs." Grandma said matter-of-factly. She sat on the recliner and motioned with her cane for me to join her on the adjacent matching couch.

"And no, an agent is like a police informant. They're not actually employed by the agency, but report to a case officer, like me. But I started off as an analyst, then transferred to National Clandestine Services."

"You mean where the spies work?" I asked.

She nodded. "Then I promoted to Targeting Officer. I spent most of my time in DC before being transferred overseas. That wasn't easy. I was disparaged for having a two-year-old at home, but no one criticized my male counterparts. When I joined the agency, they encouraged all women into analyst positions. My goal was operations. I wasn't about to let six years of college go to waste."

"How long were you in the CIA?"

"Thirty-two years. I was twenty-five-years-old, fresh out of college and finished at fifty-seven. I had a wonderful career." She stared into space. "I knew when I was eighteen, after Kennedy was assassinated, what I wanted to do. I started during Watergate and ended shortly after 9/11."

Grandma was in a trancelike state as she spoke. "I lost a lot of friends in the Towers. When thousands were dead and everyone's in a panic, I had to figure out how to stop the next bomb from coming. Emotions were put aside and after a while I became numb. Although it's been eighteen years since I left, I still wake every morning looking for information that might be a precursor to something bigger. It takes a while to step back from the intensity."

"Ah, hence all the TVs and your ... com center," I said. "What did Grandpa think of it all?"

"Dickie?" She beamed from ear to ear. "I met him in the Air Force. He was a pilot, and I was assigned to linguistics and studied French, Arabic, and German." She laughed. "That piqued his interest. The Agency recruited me and your grandfather at the same time."

She picked up his picture that sat on the

table next to her chair, gazed at it. "We were what they called a tandem couple. It's CIA term for married spies. It wasn't without danger. We were stationed, well, I can't tell you the locations." She winked. "But your grandpa was on a terrorist hit list. We drove in armored Humvees and had guards outside our flat. Every morning they'd walk around the vehicle with a mirrored stick to make sure we wouldn't go up in smoke."

She sighed and put back the picture. "There's more. But that's a story for another time." She looked to the heavens as tears dropped down her high cheek bones. "I miss him every day. I have a standing appointment with him."

"Not too soon, Gran. And I know what you mean. That's another thing we have in common." I stared at my wedding ring as I twisted it around my finger. "Does it ever get any easier?" I asked.

"No, but you learn to live with it, and it stops hurting as much. And then you wake up one day, able to breathe again." She wiped her face.

"How long has it been, Gran?" I asked.

"Fifteen years. He died in a plane crash. I think he was bumped off ... again a story—"

"For another time." I shot her a tight smile.

"How about Bradley?" she asked.

"A few months ago. He was murdered too." I let out an exaggerated sigh. "My Bradley and Mom died within three months of one another. It pretty much sucked. Everyone keeps telling me to move on, get help, blah blah blah. It doesn't work that way. And then when I tried to convince everyone that numb nuts was following me." I jutted my chin to the interrogation room. "They want to commit me."

"I believe you, sweetie." She smiled. "Okay. Story time is over, we've got work to do." Grandma eased to a stand on her cane.

CHAPTER 39

"It's all done. And there ain't no loose ends." Maggie huffed. "But we only took care of two of your ladies."

"What? I can't understand you. What are you doing?" Thomas said.

"Packing. We're fixin' to leave. But first, I want the rest of our money," Maggie demanded.

"Excuse me! Your job is not finished," Thomas snapped as he motored his Nautique Super Air G25. It was a new purchase, and he was taking it for a spin around Flathead Lake. "Where is Rose?"

"I told you. Rose didn't come, she's with family or shit. Don't know where she went."

Thomas pulled the phone away from his ear and rolled his neck. "Where. The. Hell. Is. My.

Painting?" Thomas asked slowly through gritted teeth.

"I. Do. Not. Know," she replied in kind. "Rose might have it with her, it ain't in the lodge. Rebel and me looked. You put trackers on all the cars, look for yourself," Maggie snarled.

Thomas turned red as he handed the boat's wheel over to Crockett. He didn't trust anyone with his laptop and had it with him at all times.

"Hmm ... someone disabled it in Darby. What the hell is going on down there? Your job is far from done. And I will not pay you until such time. And ... where is Heidi?"

"She stayed behind reading or knitting or whatever old people do."

"Keep your eyes on her. If she leaves, follow her. I want to know where she is at *all* times." Thomas pressed end on his cell.

He dialed another number. "When are you arriving? I've got another job for you," he grumbled.

"I'm here, now," Shilo said.

"Stay put. I need you to do something." He disconnected.

"Crock, if you want something done right, you've got to do it yourself." Thomas resumed piloting the boat.

"That's right, boss," Crockett said.

"Call your cousin, Dale. Have him charter a Cessna. The Ravalli Airport cannot accommodate my Stream." Thomas sighed and rolled his eyes.

He motored his boat to the dock where Shilo

stood waving and grinning. He always had a Plan B and sometimes a Plan C. And this woman greeting him would give her right arm for Thomas. He knew it.

CHAPTER 40

Saki woke to a blood-curdling scream. She found her sister lying on the cold dirt floor of the root cellar, an arm's length away. She groaned and blinked, hoping to clear the fog from her brain.

"It's okay, just ketamine," Saki slurred and widened her eyes.

The flickering light from the lantern their captors left behind illuminated the terror on Kaylee's face. She couldn't speak and stared. She muttered, "Body."

"Huh?" Saki tried to roll over but couldn't. She looked up and discovered her arms were above her head too, wrists bound with handcuffs. Gav had attached the cuffs to a belt that wrapped around the same metal pipe as Kaylee's restraints.

"Look," Kaylee said, eyes wide.

Saki peered down. "Holy Shit ... mother fucker," she shouted and shut her eyes as if the dead body lying at her feet would disappear. She quickly returned her attention to Kaylee. "I'm sorry. It's okay. We got this." Her heart pounded out of her chest at her weak attempt to calm her sister.

Kaylee still could not form a sentence and stared with a gaped mouth at Gav. Gav with a neat hole in his forehead, wide eyes, and a shocked expression on his face.

Saki donkey-kicked the body as far away from her as possible. But her legs were also bound with zip ties. Being restrained was not an unfamiliar experience but having a dead guy at her feet was a first.

"Okay, Kaylee, we're gonna get out of this. But first you need to focus on me. Don't look at him. He got what he deserved."

Kaylee nodded and shivered, eyes trained on her sister.

Rose was the cool, collected one of them and had bailed Saki out of many crazy situations. Now it was her turn to be the big sister, the rescuer.

"Sweetie, you have to focus. Please. This is what you have to do." Her voice was low and steady. "You see the belt above my head? It's close to your hands. I need you to unbuckle it."

Kaylee's hands shook as she fumbled. "It's hard to see." She muttered her first words.

"I know, just feel for it. You almost got it." Saki wiggled her wrists.

"Okay." Kaylee whimpered.

"There you go ... perfect." Saki raised her voice.

After Kaylee removed the belt, the room went black. Kaylee screamed again.

"It's okay, Sis. The lantern's out." Saki brought her cuffed hands down to her waist and suddenly remembered her warming jacket's battery was also a flashlight. She scooted over to Kaylee and detached it.

"Oh, thank you, husband. Now I need to find something sharp." She shone the light around the dank, musty room. And there she found it, sticking out of Gav's jeans pocket.

"I knew the shit bird would have something," Saki mumbled as she army crawled to his body and took the folding knife from his front pocket and opened the blade.

She cut the zip ties and freed her legs. Saki tried to remove the cuffs with the knife but cut herself. "Crap!" She looked around the room for another avenue. "I got it!" She squealed so loud Kaylee jumped.

"What?"

"Some girls' sisters teach them about make-up and guys. Not mine. Rose taught me how to get out of handcuffs. She made me practice over and over until I became a pro." Saki handed the jacket battery to Kaylee. "Here, hold the light."

Saki lifted her shirt and held the hem under her chin.

"What are you doing?" Kaylee asked.

Saki didn't respond. She cut a small slit on

the inside of her bra and removed the under wire. She then inserted it into the keyhole in the cuffs and continued to twist it until she was able to pick the lock and free herself.

"Oh my gosh. Rose taught you that?" Kaylee almost laughed.

"Yep. I went through so many bras. Okay ... now it's your turn." Saki removed her sister's handcuffs.

Kaylee rubbed her wrists and shook her hands.

They grappled with Kaylee's ankle restraints, with no success. Gav had attached the shackles to the same pipe, but with a long chain.

Saki ran outside and came back with a sharp-edged rock and pummeled the chain. It was useless. She let out a heavy sigh and lowered her head. "I'm so sorry, Kaylee. I have to run for help." She stood.

"No! Please don't leave me here. Not with ... him." She plead and stared at the body. "Sorry, I've done autopsies, but I never saw a fresh one." She grimaced.

"I'm taking his nasty ass out of here." Saki pulled Gav by his ankles and dragged him outside the cellar. Moments later, she returned to Kaylee.

"I promise I will get you out of here. This is a battery-operated heating jacket. It has ten hours of heat, maybe less now." Saki re-attached the battery to the jacket. "Use spar ..." The room spun and Saki stumbled backward.

"Sis, you don't look so good. The ketamine is still in your system. Did you eat anything today?" Kaylee asked.

"No, but I'm fine." She shook her head, removed the water bottle from her pocket, and took a sip. She handed the bottle to Kaylee.

As Kaylee leaned over, a brown bag fell from Saki's coat pocket.

"Hey, I forgot about that," Saki said. She took a couple bites of the breakfast bagel and gave Kaylee the rest.

"I have to go, but I promise to get you help." She patted Kaylee's legs. "You're cold." Saki ran outside again and returned with Gav's coat.

"No." Kaylee shook her head. "No way am I wearing a dead man's jacket."

"Come on, you need it. He doesn't. You have to stay warm, you're not moving your body." She gave Kaylee her best *Big Sister in Charge* look. "There's also warming gloves in the inside pocket." Saki sighed. "I love you." And hugged her.

"I love you too. If anything happens ... I'm glad we found one another." Kaylee lowered her gaze.

"Don't! Do not say that ... we are going to survive this, I promise." Saki flipped the hood over her head and bolted out of the cellar.

She peered at her watch. It was only four o'clock, but the sun was starting its descent behind the mountain. Saki had a bit over two hours before nightfall.

She thought time was on her side.

CHAPTER 41

"He's slowly coming to ... sheesh, how much did you give him, Griz?"

"Enough to get the job done." Griz smirked as he leaned back on one of the metal chairs with his hands behind his head.

I towered over Titos and flicked his nose. "I'll bet he was a handsome gent at one point." I grabbed his face and turned it left and then right, examining his worn features.

"Wha? Where the fuck am I?" Titos slurred and snapped awake.

"How does it feel ... *Princess*?" I snatched a water bottle from the table and sprayed his face.

"You know that's not how water boarding works." Griz mocked.

"You're a funny guy." I gave him a half-raspberry.

I squirted Titos again.

"I'm not a cat," he growled as he peered at his restraints.

It reminded me of a scene from a Frankenstein movie.

"I thought you were dead. Does Satan know you've escaped?" I tapped his forehead.

"Yeah, he gave me a fuckin' hall pass to come get you." He snarled and thrust forward, but the leather straps held him back. The weight of his body caused the gurney to roll a couple inches.

Griz ran up and adjusted the wheel brakes.

"Easy tiger, you're going to get hurt." I tightened the straps.

"What are you doing to me?" he shrieked.

"We couldn't strap you to a chair on account of … you know." I scanned his hook and leg. "Your missing body parts." I snickered.

"Yeah, thanks to you and Max. Look at me, I'm half a man," he shouted and flung his head forward again.

"Seriously? You are blaming *me*? You brought this …" I danced my fingers in the air over his body. "On yourself." I pursed my lips and crossed my arms. "Hmm … you and Max murdered my husband, shot my parolee, who then shot me." I drew closer to his face and was inches from his nose. "I can't fully extend my left arm." I stood up and showed him my limitations.

"You then sacked my house, beat me up in a flea-bag motel in the Keys, shot my partner and left him for dead in the swamps." I took in a deep breath. "Excuse me if I don't attend your *fucking pity party!*" I raised my good arm and slapped his face into Idaho.

Grandma must have been watching from the other side because within seconds she interrupted my fun and held me back.

Griz sat with a Cheshire grin and watched the show.

"Take that crazy bitch out of here," Titos shouted.

"Go to hell," I screamed back as the veins in my neck pulsed.

"My room ain't ready," Titos retorted.

Just as I raised my hand again, Grandma ushered me into the war room and closed the door. "We won't get any answers from him this way." Grandma patted my arm as Griz followed.

"Well, that's one way of releasing your anger." Lily sat on a bar stool and leaned forward as she peered into the room.

"Was that too much?" I scrunched my face and gave her a sideways glance.

"It was righteous." Griz flashed me a cheeky grin and gave me a fist bump.

"I hate to admit it, but it felt kinda good," I said.

"Honey, there're times your tactics have to be less than honorable to get to the truth."

"Grandma, my honor went out the window this morning," I said.

"Like I said, that won't work. He's accustomed to a punch in the face. This is not

Titos's first rodeo," Grandma said.

"As the rider or the clown?" I snarled.

Griz opened the drawer and pulled out what looked like a cattle prod.

"What the heck?" My eyes bulged.

Grandma shot Griz a look and back to me.

"He already knows how a taser feels. But not this. You'll see," she replied with a calm, eerie tone.

CHAPTER 42

After the rocking and rolling stopped, James assessed his surroundings. He was suspended upside down and the sun was setting behind the mountain. He looked at Kevin, who appeared to be drifting in and out of consciousness. More in than out.

"You okay?" James asked.

"Mmm. I'm alive. Thank God." Kevin touched his head where the blood had been pouring down his face onto the steering wheel.

"Don't move, buddy." James removed his seat belt and slid out of the SUV. He ran to Kevin's side, but the belt was jammed. He took his knife from his camouflage pants' side pocket and cut Kevin loose. He braced his neck and gently rolled him out and leaned him against a bolder.

James looked around for his black medic bag and found it a few feet away, alongside the satellite phone. He retrieved both and returned to Kevin. He removed a roll of gauze and applied pressure to his friend's oozing head wound, and closely examined it. "Not too bad. Any dizziness?" James asked.

"We just rolled a mile down a freaking cliff, of course I'm dizzy." He snuffled.

"Copy that, stupid question." James chuckled.

"Sorry, no, I'm good. I've had a concussion before, and I am sure this is mild. Thanks, pal." Kevin gave him a closed-mouth smile as James wrapped the bandage around his head and wiped the blood from his face.

"Hmpf, I forgot you were a boy scout and a medic. Always prepared," Kevin said.

"Yeah." James snickered "Okay, let's look at you. Anything broken, other than your pride?" He offered his hand to Kevin.

"No." He stood and peered up the hillside and then back to the crumpled SUV. He stared at James. "Our brake lines were cut," Kevin said.

"Yeah, that's what I thought. And did you notice? No airbags. They must've been disabled." James touched his pockets.

"Looking for this?" Kevin picked up his cell phone that was lying next to the SUV and handed it to him.

"Gotta love these military grade cases." James held the phone in the air. "But no service. Let me try the sat." James scampered around, searching for a signal on the satellite phone.

"You know, we can make it." Kevin looked at James and nodded up the hill.

"Hmm. There's a fresh layer of snow, may be too icy ... hey, I got through." After James told the dispatcher their accident and location, he was informed help would arrive as soon as possible. There was another rescue going on and the county was shorthanded.

"Screw it, let's go for it," Kevin said after James disconnected.

An hour later, the guys made it to the top of the hill just as a Ravalli County Sheriff's Deputy pulled in followed by a fire truck.

"Are you all right?" The uniformed deputy approached the men.

"We're alive." James looked back to Kevin. "But my friend here has a head wound."

"I'm fine, you know how head wounds are, they're worse than they look." Kevin gave a wobbly smile. "Our vehicle, that's another story." He motioned down at the wreckage.

"I have an ambulance on the way," the deputy said.

"Please, no worries. I'm okay. Can you cancel the call?" Kevin said.

"Copy that." The deputy stepped away and returned a couple minutes later. "I'm Deputy Jake Kass, but call me Jake."

Jake stood James's height with a black close-trimmed beard and in addition to his deputy uniform, he wore a black felt cowboy hat and black Ariat boots.

Kevin and James made their introductions.

"That's right, Sheriff Horton mentioned you gentlemen were in town. He told me to keep an eye out for you all and extend a Ravalli County welcome." Jake tipped his hat and peered down the hill. "And this is no proper welcome." He shook his head.

"Yes, Scott Horton and I go way back. We met at the FBI academy. I was teaching a class he attended. Anyway ..." Kevin retold the hair-raising chain of events as Jake wrote down the details.

"You're correct, it sounds suspicious. The vehicle will need to be inspected ... and here comes the tow truck. Once the scene is clear, I'll take you gentlemen back to town."

CHAPTER 43

It was 4:30 p.m. when James threw the lodge door open wide.

Heidi was curled up on the couch by a crackling fire reading a book titled, *Secrets in the Keys.* She jumped.

"Sorry, scary story?" James asked.

"No, just suspenseful. This is the author's first book. She's a friend of Rose, a retired parole agent." Heidi set it down and stood with her back to the fire. Her mouth dropped at the sight of him.

James's clothes were ragged and hair disheveled. His face was covered in lacerations.

"Oh my. Did the deer win?" She put her hand to her lips.

"Something like that." James set his backpack on the floor and joined her.

"Where's Kevin?" Heidi asked. Right after her inquiry, he came in with another man.

James made the introductions to Heidi.

"Wow, I'm sorry to stare, but I didn't realize law enforcement officers dress like cowboys in Montana." She gushed. "And you look just like that man from the Dun—"

"You mean, Rip? Yeah, I get that all the time. Except he looks like me." Jake winked.

James cleared his throat. "Uh, Heidi. Where are the ladies? I tried calling, but none of their phones are on, including Rose's." He crossed his arms.

"Rose turned off her phone. She left me a note saying if there was an emergency to call this number." Heidi pulled a piece of paper from her pocket and handed it to James.

"Oh. And Maggie told me she dropped the girls off downtown after fishing. I guess they wanted to go shopping?" Heidi shrugged her shoulders.

"It's Sunday, all the shops are closed. Maybe they went to eat." Jake made his way into the living room.

"No. We had dinner plans." James paced. "Heidi, where are Maggie and Rebel? I'd like a chat with them."

"Are you talking about Robert and Maggie Banks?" Jake asked.

"Yeah, why?" James replied.

"Oh boy, those two are trouble. They're from Texas. Maggie is a known felon. She was on parole for ADW, attempted murder, possession of firearms. You know, the fun stuff. Robert or

Rebel just goes along with the program. They had a rough life and were raised in the foster system. They eventually got adopted as teens to a decent family. But it was too late for Maggie. The damage was done." Jake rubbed his hands by the fire.

"Why do you know so much about them?" Kevin sat on the chair and put his head back.

"Maggie has warrants out of Louisiana and I've been trying to work with Rebel. He's not a bad fellow," Jake said.

"Yeah, for someone who sabotaged our truck." Kevin snarked.

"No, Rebel doesn't seem that sort of person. Besides, I don't think he would know how. Who was with him?" Jake pulled out his note pad, again.

"A weird guy, named Joe. No known last name." James said.

Kevin nodded. "Yeah, there was something eerie about Joe. That asshole was in a hurry to leave too." He looked at Heidi. "Sorry, ma'am."

"Oh, that's fine," Heidi said.

While Kevin told Jake all the mishaps since their arrival yesterday, James picked up his phone to call Rose. Just then an incoming text message buzzed.

"Hmm ... Daisy sent this earlier." James ran his hand through his hair as he read it.

"She did some digging and discovered Thomas Marchetti is a pseudonym. The listed owner of this lodge is under a shell company named M. Marchetti from Italy." James stopped reading and stared. He felt the blood drain from his face as he plunked on the couch. "The M stands for Madeline. She is none other than the grandmother of Maxwell Ryan, from Miami. Who now lives in Italy under the name of Thomas Marchetti." James hung his head.

"No!" Heidi let out a gasp and plopped next to James. "This can't be happening again. Not to my girls." She curled her fists. "When I get my paws on Maxwell, that little shit. He is going to wish he was never born."

James and Kevin stared at one another with raised eyebrows and didn't utter a word.

Heidi looked at them. "Oh, I am so sorry. My language. I am just sick to my stomach worried. Something has happened to them." She clasped her hands.

"I'll put out a BOLO for Maggie and Rebel," Jake said.

"BOLO?" Heidi tilted her head.

"It's cop speak for, Be On the Look Out," James said as he dialed Rose.

CHAPTER 44

"**W**h ... what are you doing?" Sweat poured out of Titos and his skin was flushed.

He'd been out of it for the better part of the day. But now he was awake.

"Hey ... I know what that is, yo ... you can't use that on me. That'll kill me. I ... I got a bad heart." His speech was pressured.

"You're dead, remember? We can't kill a dead man. And does anyone know you're missing?" I held the cattle prod in my hands.

"Hey, Lily." I pursed my lips and turned on the prod. "It's legal to bury a body on private property in Montana, right?"

"Yes," Lily replied as she stared through Titos. She tossed around a black plastic object in her hands.

"What's that for?" His eyes expanded, the whites larger than his irises.

"We don't want you biting off your tongue," Lily replied.

"You two broads are bat shit nutso."

I looked at Lily. "I've been called way worse by way better."

He growled. "Where's the old lady?"

Grandma walked in as Lily left the room.

Without saying a word, Grandma pulled up a metal chair beside Titos. She sat silent and glared at him for five minutes, repeatedly tapping her cane on the floor.

The room was still, except for Titos's shallow breathing. He gawked at the prod in my hand and shot bug-eyed glances at me and Grandma.

"This is freaking me out. Say something ... or do something, just don't stare at me like that," he spouted.

"Titos. Why are you here?" Grandma asked slowly and deliberately as she leaned forward on her cane.

"These crazy bitches abducted me," he snapped.

"*No.*" She slammed her cane and shouted. "Wrong answer."

I didn't expect that from her and jumped out of my skin.

"Titos ... why are you in Montana?" Grandma asked again in the same fashion.

"I thought I'd do a little fly fishing and hook up with a local hottie." He stared through the mirror. "I know you can see me, doll. I've stood on that side of the mirror. I was in the fucking

FBI. And what you're all doing is a crime! You're gonna pay." He jutted his chin at us.

I looked at Lily, who I assumed watched from the other side. "He is unbelievable. If he were not recorded as deceased, he'd have a list of felony charges." I rolled my head back and guffawed.

Grandma stood. "We can do this the easy, or the hard way. Your choice." The evil intent in her voice chilled the room a few degrees.

"I ain't no rat. In my hood, snitches end up as bitches." Titos swayed his head.

"Very well." Grandma nodded at the glass window. "Are you thirsty, Titos?"

"What? He doesn't deserve water," I sniped.

"No, we need to treat him humanely." She nodded to the window.

"Yeah ... that'll be great." He glared at me and shot a cheeky grin as if he won a round.

Griz entered with what I assumed was water and a straw.

Titos stared at the glass. "Hey, I'm not falling for that again. Sweet cheeks in there gave me shit last night and this morning."

"You can smell it if you want," Grandma said calmly.

He peered into the glass and sniffed it. "Okay." And slurped it all down.

I let out a heavy sigh and furrowed my brows. "I'd rather use the prod."

Grandma looked at her watch. "Anytime now."

"Hmm?" I squinted at her.

"SP-117. A Russian truth serum that works

better than sodium pentothal. It's odorless, colorless, no immediate side effects. After our chat, he will think he fell asleep."

Titos stared without saying a word.

"How did you get ... never mind." I shook my head.

"And if that doesn't work, we use our little friend here as encouragement." Grandma nodded to the prod in my hands.

I flinched as the burner phone in my back pocket buzzed.

Grandma stared at me.

"I only gave it to Heidi for an emergency. I need to take it." I stepped inside the war room.

My nostrils flared and jaws clenched as James recounted his morning in great detail, including my missing sisters.

As I spoke with him, Grandma shook her head at me. I guess Titos was tougher than the SP-117.

"James, we're all up shit creek. I'm in a bit of a situation myself. I'll call you right back." The eerie calmness in my voice frightened me. "I'm going to get some answers."

CHAPTER 45

A red-hot cloak constricted my neck as I burst open the door and made a beeline to Titos. I put the cattle prod on medium setting and gave him a zap, without the comforts of his mouthpiece.

Grandma did not say a word. She took a step back and motioned for Griz to do the same.

"Fuuuck," Titos shouted.

"Next time it will be stronger. Now, *where the hell are they*?" My shout blew his hair back.

I looked at Grandma and repeated the conversation with James.

"I know you're working for Max, that dirty mother! He set this whole trip up ... but why?" I seethed through gritted teeth.

"Yes, at first, I was, but I swear he doesn't know I'm here," Titos pled.

"Where are my sisters?"

Suddenly Titos's eyes glazed over, and he laughed.

"Hmm, that's an unusual side effect, and it took it a little longer to work," Grandma said.

"What would your partner, the boy scout, think of your interrogation technique?" he asked with a shit-eating grin. "Not exactly by the book."

"Sometimes bad behavior makes people listen. And besides, he's no longer my partner. I'm probably without a job, so I couldn't give a rat's ass what anyone thinks. Now tell me, where they are." I twisted his hook.

"Hey ... take it easy, Rose." He bobbled his head. "You know you're kinda sexy when you're pissed. Whatcha say you untie me, and I'll give you a night to remember." His Bronx accent all but took over his dialect.

I turned the cattle prod on a stronger setting and zapped him again.

"*Argh!*" Titos hollered. The last time I heard him scream like that he was in the swamps.

"Okay ... okay. You take the fun out of it, jeezo. Max is unloading a couple paintings. And you know sumtin' else? That piece of fuck changed his name to Thomas and dyed his hair. He thinks he can hide. Pshh. He's at his lake house in Whitefish." Titos grinned again. "You see, Crock and me are gonna take off wit one of em. We deserve it."

"I don't care." I pounded the wall and shook my head at Grandma. "That's not the information I asked for ... now where the hell are Kaylee and Saki?"

"I swear, all I know is Max hired a crazy brother-sister team from Texas to take 'em fishin' and get rid of them. You gotta know Max is crazy for you and he thinks you're gonna marry him." Titos struggled to keep his eyes open.

I let out an exaggerated sigh and paced. After a couple seconds I blurted, "Grandma, I need your computer."

We went inside and Grandma unlocked her computer again with her fingerprint scanner.

I called James, put him on speaker and told him who was in the room. But left Titos out of the equation.

I clicked away at the keyboard and entered a website.

"You have a tracker on your sister's phone?" Grandma asked.

"Don't judge." I kept my attention on the screen.

"No. I'm impressed. That's my gal." Grandma patted my back.

"Whatcha got for me, Rose?" James asked.

"This is Saki's last known location ... right here." I pointed the cursor and glanced at Grandma. "Kaylee also sent a selfie from that general vicinity."

"That's a few miles down the road to the west." Lily chimed in as she looked over my shoulder.

"We have one deputy. Sheriff Horton can't spare anyone else right now. The search and rescue team are all tied up too," James said.

I looked around the room at my crew. "That should be plenty."

"We need air support. A helicopter would be ni—never mind, negative on the chopper. Jake said they don't have any available on such short notice," James said.

Grandma whispered she had a chopper and just as she was about to say the word "pilot," Tubbs entered the room.

"I've got that covered too." I gave Uncle Tubbs a feeble grin.

CHAPTER 46

Thomas touched down at the Ravalli County Airport at six p.m. He wasn't impressed with the Cessna Dale rented, but it was a mere thirty-eight-minute flight and it beat the three and a half hours it would have taken to drive from Kalispell.

The second Dale turned off the plane, Thomas's phone rang. He peeked at the caller ID.

"What," he barked.

"The sheriffs are at the lodge. I'm sure they are looking for us," Maggie shouted on the other end of the call.

"How would they know of your involvement, unless the loose ends were not tied?" Thomas seethed.

"Uh ... why else would they be here and I

kinda got warrants out of Louisiana."

"Something you failed to disclose." He ran his hands through his hair. Thomas knew a thing or two about warrants, since he, a.k.a., Max had a list a mile long, with federal kidnapping charges at the top.

"Of course, I didn't mention it to you. You weren't looking for Harvard graduates, now were you ... ah, shit, I gotta call Rebel. If they catch him, he'd sing like a dumbass bird. We gotta split tonight ... I want the rest of my money," Maggie demanded.

"Your job is not finished." Thomas hung up and dialed another number.

"Things have gone from bad to worse. My lackeys in Hamilton are out of the equation. It's Plan B time. They'll all be busy looking for the sisters, no one will be watching the old lady. Bring her to me. I just texted you the address to the ranch. And don't fuck this up or I swear it'll be the last thing you ever do."

As he disconnected the call, Crockett arrived on the tarmac in one of the Escalades.

"It's about damn time. Where the hell have you been?" Thomas glared at him.

"Hey. You told me to get the other house ready, so I did." Crockett acknowledged his cousin Dale with a nod.

Dale exited the cockpit and opened Thomas's door.

Thomas's phone rang again. Chena. He ignored the call.

CHAPTER 47

I hung up and rushed into Tubbs's arms. My stomach was twisted in triple knots. "It's all my fault Kaylee is missing." I let out a strangled sob. "I'm so sorry. Max is after me. Not them," I said.

"Look at me, Rosie." He released my arms. "We're going to find them," Tubbs said as his brown eyes gave me a reassuring gaze.

I felt safe with him, in a fatherly manner. "Yes ... we have a great team here. The guys are on their way." I shoved my inner helpless little girl aside. We had work to do.

"Here's what we have so far." Grandma pulled down a map of the valley. "The last known location of Saki's phone was here." She pointed. "There's not much out there but forest. We don't know where or how far they got, or ..." She looked around the room. "Their condition."

My heart skipped a few beats hearing those words fall from her mouth, but it was the truth and sometimes the truth hurts.

"It's tough terrain, and not accessible by motored vehicle." Grandma showed us on the map. "My helicopter may help, but the forest is thick with pines and firs."

"I got it!" Lily exclaimed. "I've been riding out there, and I've seen an abandoned root cellar. It could be the only place to put a bo—" She caught herself. "I mean to—"

"It's okay, Lily." Griz placed his hand on her shoulder. "We know what you mean. And we'll find them."

"Griz and I will saddle up the horses and take the dogs, Rose can go in the chop—"

"No. I'm riding too." They all stared at me. "Saki and I rode every week when we lived in San Diego, and I still ride. I've got this ... and those are my sisters out there." I punctuated the last four words with fist slams on the table.

Grandma stood. "Okay, it's settled. The three of you go by horseback. Kevin and James can go with Tubbs in the chopper." Grandma stood tall as she put her team together.

"I can also use my drone. We'll be able to fly lower than the helicopter," Lily said. "It's equipped with night vision."

"Wow." Griz nudged her. "You never cease to amaze me. Mounted shooting, wrangling, now drone expert. I'm impressed, Sister."

"Perfect," I said. "Thanks, Lily. Now, uh ... what about him?" I nodded to Titos.

"He's your fish, what do you want me to do with him?" Grandma raised her brows.

"I've got all the information I need. I'm done and don't care. He's all yours. Make him disappear." I spoke with a stone expression.

"That's not how this game works. You catch 'em, you clean 'em." Grandma leaned forward on her cane. "Tell me."

I whispered in her ear.

"Copy." She smirked.

We marched up the stairs to prepare for our rescue mission.

CHAPTER 48

A cold, winter-like breeze chilled Saki's bones. She'd been warned about the rapid fluctuation in weather patterns in Montana and was prepared until Kaylee needed her jacket more.

Although she was an avid outdoorsman and long-distance runner, the ketamine lingered in her system. Saki quickly became disoriented as she sprinted downhill, stumbling as often as she ran. The wind kicked up a notch and howled through the trees. A sudden eerie calm fell in the air and the wind shifted.

As daylight all but disappeared behind the mountains, Saki was positive she passed the same outcropping of trees. Everything looked the same. The further she traversed, the thicker the forest grew. The adage, *can't see the forest through the trees,* made sense to her.

Did she go in the right direction? She couldn't be certain. Her heart pounded faster and louder with each stride. Suddenly, the sound of branches breaking startled her. She stopped in her tracks, held her breath and stood frozen in the darkness. *Bears!*

She exhaled a sigh of relief when a doe ran across her path, so Saki kept moving, but the high altitude was too much for her to handle.

The woods spun out of control. "No, you have to stay strong." She grabbed her face. The sound of a babbling creek beckoned. She ran over, cupped the water into her hands and took a sip. She shot up with a gasp. "That's it, I'll follow the stream." The half-moon glistening off the water provided a little extra light for her.

As Saki stepped over jagged rocks and dodged low-hanging branches, she scolded herself. If only she'd cancelled the fishing trip, they would be sitting by the fire, drinking hot cocoa. *Always trust your instincts,* Rose would say. But Maggie had ushered her out of the house so quickly, not giving her a chance to argue.

"I am going to kick that witch's ass when I see her." Anger sizzled like an erupting volcano and she screamed as loud as she could, but her breathing labored.

The forest swirled again, and she fell to her knees. *Keep moving, Saki, don't stop.* Out of nowhere a quote from the book of Romans popped in her head. It was her mother's favorite scripture: *Suffering provides perseverance; perseverance character; and character hope.*

Saki's cognition ebbed as she swore the angel of her mother hovered over her. The angel peered down and smiled upon her. Saki reached out her hand, but it vanished. Her first aid training told her hallucinations are a sign of hypothermia.

She squeezed her eyes tight and used her remaining strength to get to her feet, but her legs gave way and she collapsed.

Black spots danced across Saki's eyes and her vision narrowed.

CHAPTER 49

It took twenty minutes for Lily and Griz to load the trailer with the horses and pack mule. It was obviously not their first rescue mission, so their supplies were ready to go.

We were equipped with flashlights, radios, blankets, first aid kit, MREs, and extra water, just in case it turned into an overnighter. Griz and Lily each carried a shotgun and side arms. And since the only weapon in my arsenal was my compact 9 mm, Grandma loaned me her Marlin .45-70 lever action rifle.

Even Stevo and Brian were adorned with lighted collars and vests.

"Hold on." Lily hurried inside and returned with her black felt cowboy hat. "There, that's better." She grinned and put it on my head.

I nodded and managed a smile as I adjusted

the brim.

Kevin and James drove up just after we loaded the last bit of equipment into Lily's Dodge Ram. James advised that Deputy Jake was meeting us at the West Fork boat launch with his horse. He also contacted the ER and had them on stand-by.

Tubbs had the chopper ready to go when the guys arrived, so they jumped in with him and flew west along the river.

It was ten minutes shy of seven when we reached the rally point. The temperature dropped at least ten degrees as a winter-like storm rolled into the Valley. The moon all but hid behind clouds now. Jake had arrived moments before us and was inspecting a fishing raft that was pulled up along the shore of the river, just east of the Job Corp facility. "This must be theirs, your sisters'." He peered up at me.

A lump developed in my throat and my bottom lip quivered.

"Don't worry. We'll find them." Lily patted my arm.

After the horses and mule were led out of the trailer, we headed over the bridge across the river with the dogs at our sides. Ten minutes into the ride, Brian stopped with his nose in the air.

Lily held her hand up to halt our movement. "He's got something. Brian is a cadaver dog."

Cadaver dog? My heart ached at the thought.

We followed Brian over the hill as he tracked

a scent, while Stevo remained on guard duty.

"He found someone," Lily said.

Upon our arrival, Brian sat and alerted to what appeared to be a body lying on the ground.

God, please don't let this be one of my sisters. I prayed hard.

"Let me look," I pled and dismounted the horse.

"I'm going, too. It's my county." Jake hopped off his gelding.

"Yes, of course." I nodded and removed the Marlin from the leather scabbard as Jake and I made our way to the body.

Lily followed and rewarded Brian for his find.

Jake looked first and rolled the body over. "It's a man," he said. "A local tweaker named Gav."

I looked to the heavens and breathed a sigh of relief.

All was quiet for a second and then a female shouted, "Help me. Please. I'm in the root cellar."

"I know that voice. It's Kaylee." My heart somersaulted.

Lily gave Brian and Stevo hand signals and they galloped toward Kaylee's voice. Lily stayed with the horses.

I followed the dogs and ran as quick as my feet would carry me with Griz on my heels.

The second we hit the cellar entrance, we found Kaylee in leg shackles.

"Oh my God! Thank you, thank you!" she

wailed.

Stevo and Brian were already inside, wagging their tails and slobbering Kaylee with kisses.

I ran up and embraced her.

She shivered as she told me Saki's warming jacket battery died about an hour ago.

"We're getting you out of here, Sis," I said.

Griz and I pried at the shackles, but it was futile.

"I have something that might work." Griz bolted from the cellar.

"I am so glad Saki found her way out," Kaylee said with a weak smile.

"I'd hoped she was here with you." My voice dropped to a whisper. I held her body close to mine and rubbed her arms.

"Oh my God! *No.* She left a while ago." Kaylee pulled away from me.

My heart sank.

I was thankful the darkness hid the terror that had to be on my face.

CHAPTER 50

Heidi paced the lodge, waiting for word of a successful rescue. Since she insisted on staying in the event her girls showed, James agreed, with the stipulation she had security. So a wrangler named Andy, a close acquaintance of Jake's, sat with her.

As Heidi peered out the window for the umpteenth time, Andy received a call from a friend who worked dispatch.

"Maggie and Rebel were taken in for questioning about an hour ago." Andy relayed the message.

A moment of relief fell over Heidi.

"I'll be right back. Mother Nature calls. That elk stew did not agree with me." Andy held his stomach. "Here's my Mossberg. It's a pump-action shotgun." Andy showed her the mechanics. "Just don't answer the door and you shouldn't need to use it," he said.

Heidi nodded.

Moments later, a car zoomed down the driveway. Heidi stood by the window with shotgun in hand.

The driver of the vehicle got out and knocked.

"Hmm, Rose's doctor from California. Why is she here?" Heidi murmured as she walked to the door.

"Yesss?" She spoke through the screen.

"Hi. Heidi, isn't it?" the lady with red hair asked.

Heidi stood with her mouth agape and nodded. *She looks like Rose.*

"I'm Shilo, a friend of Rose's. I have some ne—"

"I know who you are. You're not her friend, but that psychologist ... what are you doing here?" Heid held the shotgun on her.

"Whoa ... easy there." Shilo waved one hand of surrender, while the other was in her jacket pocket. "I promise, I'm not a threat. I know where the gals are being held. Please, I'm begging you, let me help." Shilo tilted her head.

"Let me see your other hand," Heidi demanded as the Mossberg trembled beneath her grip as she tried unsuccessfully to pull the lever.

"Okay ... okay, just don't shoot. Take it easy." Shilo eased her hand up to the screen door and within a millisecond flung it wide.

"Help!" Heidi cried.

Shilo lunged at Heidi and disarmed her with one hand, tossing the gun on the living room floor.

"Please, don't hurt me." She hoped Andy heard her shout for help. But he must've been at the far end of the lodge.

Heidi pulled away, but Shilo grabbed her waist and held her in a death grip.

Shilo quickly produced a needle and jabbed Heidi's neck.

Her body went limp, and her legs gave way.

CHAPTER 51

Griz and I freed Kaylee with bolt cutters and exited the cellar as Jake ended his radio transmission with dispatch.

Another deputy is coming up the hill right now to take over the scene. I'll take Kaylee's statement from her, but it's getting dark, and the temps are dropping. We need to find Saki ... and soon," Jake said.

I lowered my gaze and sighed as I mounted the horse.

Kaylee said she was stable and insisted on going. She would know, she was the doc of the family. So Jake agreed to have her as his rider. He wrapped her in blankets and helped her on the horse.

The four of us split up in two different directions. Lily and I headed southeast along the stream, Jake and Griz ventured northeast, with the mule in tow.

Tubbs started in our direction, but Lily told them she couldn't fly the drone in the chopper's air space, so they backed off and continued west.

Stevo and Brian sensed the urgency and stuck to Lily. I nicknamed her the Dog Whisperer.

I heard Griz calling Saki's name in the distance, while Lily remained silent and concentrated on flying her drone. It was state-of-the-art with up to fifteen minutes of flight time when the night vision was in use. The drone was also equipped with low noise propellers.

Ten minutes went by and all was eerily silent until Lily yelled, "Stop!"

We halted the horses, and I held my breath.

"Crap, I see a black bear up ahead by the stream." Lily peered down at the dogs. "Sitz." Brian and Stevo simultaneously sat at attention.

Shivers ran down my body. "What do we do? Can we scare him away with the drone?" My speech was low and rapid.

Dealing with criminals was one thing I was good at, bears not so much.

"I've never done that, plus we don't know Saki's location. It could push the bear toward her." Lily continued to view the animal on her built-in controller screen.

She flew in closer to the stream. "Oh boy. There's a person down there, just a few feet from the bear. We gotta go." She commanded the dogs, and they were on the move.

I radioed Jake and Griz and they headed our direction.

By the time we drew near enough to see her, the bear had approached Saki.

She opened her eyes and stared at us and back to the bear. She didn't speak, and her breathing was shallow. She appeared to nod off again.

"Crap, we have to get to her." I raised my Marlin, but I didn't have a clear shot.

The bear moved closer to Saki and raised its massive paw over her body.

"Voraus," Lily said. That was Stevo and Brian's cue. They advanced.

The bear stood on her hind legs and clacked her teeth, huffing at us. The dogs barked and closed in on the beast until it backed away from Saki.

The sow scampered off but stopped a hundred yards away. Out of the corner of my eye, I spotted two cubs.

"Crap! Babies," I said.

The bear continued blowing sharply at us as she hit the ground with her paws until her cubs ran behind her into the forest and up a tree.

"She doesn't want to hurt us," Lily said. "She's only protecting her babies. Let's get Saki, fast."

Stevo rushed to Saki's side, giving her smooches until she responded.

"I knew you'd find me." She slurred and drifted.

I grabbed the extra blanket from the horse, bolted to Saki's side, and dropped to my knees. "We have to hurry. She's shivering." I covered her and checked the pulse on her wrist. "It's weak. Come on, sweetie, stay with me," I pleaded as I held her close to my body for warmth.

She whispered in my ear something about angels.

Griz and Jake arrived as the bears disappeared into the woods.

Jake radioed Tubbs, but there was no place for them to land so we agreed to meet at Grandma's.

Kaylee, Jake, and Griz dismounted their horses and Griz quickly removed his saddle.

Kaylee ran to her sister's side and examined Saki.

"Hypothermia," Kaylee said. "Not helped that she still has some ketamine in her system."

Griz took extra blankets from the pack mule and tightly wrapped Saki. He picked up her weak, limp body off the ground and laid her over the horse.

"No saddle?" I asked.

"The horse's body will help keep her warm. I'll come back for the saddle later. Besides, our vehicles are close."

We mounted the horses and took off for the truck. On the way, I glanced up and could have sworn I saw my mother's spirit hovering over Saki. I shook my head. My mind playing tricks on me. Again.

A few minutes later, Saki was prone in the

back seat of Jake's truck with the dogs quietly attentive, while he and Griz stayed behind and loaded the horses and mule into Lily's trailer.

On the twelve-minute drive to Grandma's, I held Saki close to my body and rocked her. The second we arrived at the entrance, the gates were opened, and the chopper was waiting.

James did not even let the truck stop before he'd flung the rear door open. He snatched Saki from my embrace and carried his wife's unresponsive, near-lifeless body. He was in full-blown medic mode.

I'd never seen James so panic stricken. But I imagined he was this way when he found me shot and bleeding out a few months ago.

I dropped my head.

At this moment, nothing else mattered. All my petty problems were unimportant. All that was dear and precious was in the arms of my brother-in-law.

I picked up my head and wiped my tears.

This would end tonight.

CHAPTER 52

"Wha' hap ... where am I?" Heidi's words were breathy and inaudible. Her eyelids flickered and her head bobbled as she stirred. As the world came into focus, she saw a crackling fire. She looked down and discovered she was lying on a soft leather couch.

"We are at the Stock Ranch in a suite." Thomas sat across from her in a matching chair. He leaned over to her.

"Maxwell, is that you? I ... I didn't recognize you." She peered at her watch, but her vision was out of focus.

"It's eight o'clock. And by the way, my name is Thomas now. My apologies for the ketamine. It's quick acting, with less respiratory sedation. You might hallucinate and see double, but don't worry, it's not permanent. Besides, would you have come any other way?" Thomas cocked his head.

Heidi furrowed her brows. "You should be ashamed of yourself." She scolded as she pulled herself upright to sit. "You can't get away with this. You'll be arrested for all your wrongdoings."

"We shall see. And you're lucky you're a second mother to me, or I wouldn't tolerate this back talk." His faced reddened as he made his way to the fireplace, rubbing his hands together.

"And another thing, young man." Heidi stood but fell back just as quick. "You almost killed me when you blew up Rose's car," she yelled.

Thomas snapped his head in her direction. "I swear that was not my doing! I don't know who was behind it. And I wanted no harm to come to her, she's going to be my wife someday." He ran his hands through his blond hair.

"Maxwell. You were eleven and she was seven when you made that promise to one another. For God's sake, that was twenty-three years ago."

"It's Thomas," he shouted. "And you'll see, she will grow to love me again." He stoked the fire with the poker. "Besides, she has something of mine."

"The Falcon? That was never yours. Her father bought that ... legally. And why do you care about that painting? You're a wealthy man," Heidi asked.

"I can't explain ... but it contains information worth killing for." Thomas paced and sighed.

"What are you talking about?" Heidi followed him with her eyes.

"There is a man only known as the Ghost who leaked confidential and damaging data to the Feds."

"So, what does this have to do with all of us?" Heidi raised her shoulders.

"You don't understand. Powerful and dangerous individuals have had their information exposed. That's all I can tell you. And my Rose is in the middle of it." He paced faster. "If they find out she has it, they will torture and kill her." His eyes grew wider.

"Ma ... uh, Thomas, you can't be serious. Anyway, James, Kevin, and the girls have nothing to do with it. Why involve them?"

"With her people out of the way, she'd have nobody to turn to for help but me," he said.

Just then, Shilo popped in the room.

"You ... you're a horrible person. You deserve one another." Heidi's face reddened and she stood. "Come to think of it, I'll bet money that *you* blew up Rose's car. You heard about the explosion awfully fast ... and what is with your hair. Are you trying to look like Rose?"

"You're just a crazy old woman." Shilo lunged at her.

"Is this true?" Thomas jumped in front of Shilo. "Did you have something to do with her car explosion?" He was inches from her face.

"Uh ... Thomas, darling." She backed away from him. "Rose is not worthy of your love. She doesn't appreciate you like I do. I'd do anything for you." She raised her hand to his face, but he swatted it away before she made contact. "I killed for you!"

"Don't ever touch me." He glared at her. "I never told you to murder that shrink ... uh, Dr. Brody."

She lowered her gaze and stared at the floor. Shilo turned slowly toward Heidi. "How do you plan on getting the Falcon without me?" she said with an icy tone. "And do you think Rose will take you seriously?" She spun on her heels and marched into the kitchen.

She returned moments later with a cutting board, dish towel and a butcher knife.

"What are you doing?" Thomas exclaimed.

"Rose needs to know you mean business. And I told you there's nothing I wouldn't do to prove my allegiance to you." She grabbed Heidi's hand, held it on the board and raised the knife high in the air. Shilo's eyes narrowed as she slammed the knife.

Whack!

Heidi let out an ear-piercing scream.

CHAPTER 53

Tubbs flew James and my sisters to the hospital just as Jake and Griz arrived with the trailer. Since I needed alone time, I asked Kevin to ride with Jake to Hamilton while I followed. Lily and Griz stayed behind with Grandma to attend to the animals.

On the way, I berated myself and prayed hard for my sisters and made every deal I could think of with God. Once we hit Hamilton, I jumped at a buzzing sound in the car. For a split second, I thought I was going to go *kaboom* and then realized the noise was from my personal cell. I forgot I'd powered it on once I left Grandma's secret squirrel zone.

"Yes, Kevin. I'm right behind you. Is Saki okay?" My heart skipped a few beats.

"Heidi is missing." He let out a puff of air.

"What?" A lump developed in my throat. "Jake's friend was sitting with her. How the hell did this happen?" I clutched the steering wheel with a vice grip. My hands bore the fingernail impressions.

"Jake is talking to Andy right now. We're a couple blocks from the hospital. See you there." Kevin ended the call.

Moments later I unbuckled my seat belt as I zipped into the hospital parking lot, coming to an abrupt stop. I jumped out, leaving my car running.

"Repeat that Andy, you're on speaker. Rose is here." Jake stood beside his Durango.

"I ... I don't know. I told Heidi to stay put and not answer the door, I even gave her a shotgun. I went to the bathroom and when I returned ... she was gone. The shotgun was lying on the living room floor. No signs of a struggle. I am sor—hey, a black SUV is coming down the driveway ... kinda fast," Andy said. "Who are you? What are you doing? What the hell?" Andy yelled from the other end.

"Andy, what's happening?" I asked.

"The driver threw a dark box out of the window and took off. She said it was for you, Rose."

"Wait ... don't approach it, could be a bomb," Jake shouted.

"Nah, something rolled out of it. It's wrapped in a towel ... there's blood," Andy said with a raised voice.

"Stop. Do not open the towel. Bring it to the hospital," Jake ordered.

Fifteen minutes later, Andy pulled up next to us. "Sorry. It ... it rolled out of the towel." He scrunched his face and handed Jake the box.

Jake peeked inside. "Oh. You don't want to see this." He pinched his lips.

I grabbed it and stared. "What the fuck." I gasped. I felt the blood drain out of my face.

"I can run it for fingerprints," Jake said.

Kevin took it from my hands and shook his head.

"No." I closed my eyes a brief second. "It's a lady's. I know whose it is ... that sick son of a bitch." I pounded the top of Jake's Dodge.

"Hey, here's a note." Jake handed it to me.

"Shilo. Figures ... that bitch. She left a number." I pulled out my cell and entered the digits so fast, I misdialed at first and chewed out some unsuspecting person. I dialed again.

"You psycho-bitch from hell. How dare you and Max." I looked to God and waited for lighting to strike me dead. Among my many promises to Him just minutes ago, curtailing my newfound cursing was the top of the list.

"He goes by Thomas now, and he wants you to meet him at the Ravalli County Airport in an hour. Bring the Falcons. He said *no* cops this time or you'll get Heidi back in pieces."

"Pffft ... he loves Heidi and would never harm her," I said.

"No, he wouldn't. But I would." She barked an eerie laughter.

"I want to speak to Heidi, *now*," I demanded.

"She's not feeling so well and is napping,"

Shilo replied.

"Give me proof of life," I said.

My phone buzzed. It was a picture of Heidi, hopefully just sleeping on a couch.

"One hour, alone. No tricks. He wants both Falcons."

"I need at least two hou—wait, both Falcons? What the hell does that mean? I only have one," I said.

"Two hours, no more!" *Click*. Shilo disconnected the call.

I hit redial, but it went straight to voicemail.

CHAPTER 54

I was in the middle of a tirade when James came out to the parking lot.

"What the hell? I got your text, Kevin." James sprinted to us.

"It's all my fault, AP." My voice shook as Kevin showed him the box with the pinky finger. I handed him the note and relayed my conversation with psycho Shilo.

"You are *not* in this alone." James embraced me. "Love, we all want a piece of this S.O.B."

I snapped back to why we were all there. "How are they?" I nodded to the hospital.

"Kaylee is resting. In her adrenaline surge trying to find Saki, she didn't notice her swollen ankles. But they should release her soon. Saki has hypothermia. She's exhausted and dehydrated. We're waiting on some lab test results," James said.

"I need to see them." I turned toward the hospital, but James grabbed my arm.

"They're going to be okay. Don't you have something else to do?" He looked toward Kevin.

"Okay, okay ... time is ticking. I'll jet up to Grandma's to pick up the Fal—"

"We." Kevin nudged my shoulder. "Will get the paintings. James will stay here and keep us posted. Jake needs to take this pinky to the Sheriff's Department. It's evidence." He handed it to Jake. "Remember, this is not our jurisdiction." He directed the comment to James and me.

We nodded in agreement.

"I'm going back to the station to meet with Sheriff Horton. It's a good thing he likes and trusts you guys." Jake jumped in his truck and started it. "He doesn't take kindly to outsiders wreaking havoc in his community. After you get the paintings, meet me at his office. We'll have an ops plan and the Special Response Team ready," Jake said before he sped away.

I watched James return to the hospital and then I turned to Kevin. He shot me a closed-mouth grin. "It's you and me, Red."

I shook my head and trooped back to my running vehicle.

"Hop in Agent O'Malley, the evening's about to get interesting." I slid behind the wheel and phoned Grandma.

I provided her the ghastly details and told her I had a trusted friend with me.

Kevin wore a cheeky smile when I referred to him as a *friend*. I gave her his information.

Grandma was on speaker phone when she granted Kevin's approval and said he was cleared for entry.

After I hung up, Kevin looked at me. "Cleared? I'm a Bureau Chief with the freaking FBI with a Top-level Security Clearance." He pursed his lips.

I let out an exaggerated sigh. "Yeah ... but as you well know, not all feds can be trusted. Look at Titos."

Oh, crap. I'd forgotten about Titos. Max and Shilo weren't the only ones who committed a felony today. I did as well. The reality slapped me in the face again. I was bringing in a federal agent. I looked at Kevin. He may have to arrest me too.

I said another silent prayer to the Man Upstairs. I envisioned God shaking his head and covering his eyes at my empty promises.

CHAPTER 55

It was 9:15 p.m. when we pulled into Grandma's compound. Kevin's mouth dropped open.

"Yeah, that was my reaction too. Wait until we go downstairs, you've seen nothing yet," I said.

Grandma stood outside with the dogs. Brian and Stevo received Kevin in the same manner as me. He passed their sniff test. They liked him. That was a good sign.

"I hope you gave these boys a rib eye steak dinner." The dogs turned their attention to me and greeted me like a long-lost family member. They tackled me. By the time I stood, they'd drenched my face in slobber. I didn't mind. It was a welcome distraction.

We got inside and were back to business. "So

... Grandma, what is Shilo talking about? Both Falcons?" I wrinkled my forehead.

She let out an enormous sigh. "Come with me." She motioned for Kevin and me to follow her to the war room.

As we made our way downstairs, I stood speechless. Just when I thought she could not shock me, she did. Grandma had a safe room within a safe room. It was the size of my entire master bedroom. I strode around and gawked at all the paintings. "Wh ... what the heck are these? Th ... they're all Falcons." I stared back at Kevin, who wore the same W.T.F. expression.

I approached each one and inspected them. They all looked the same. "Which is the real deal?" I drew my gaze back to her.

"None of them." Grandma leaned on her cane. "It's in protected custody."

"What?" I ran my hands through my hair. "You mean I had a forged copy?"

"No, you had the original. But, let me ask you something. Did you notice anything peculiar when you arrived at the airport yesterday?"

I cast my mind back, remembering. "As a matter of fact, I did. Tubbs ushered us away from the plane and made eye contact with another pilot. I thought it was my imagination running away with me, again."

"Good observation skills. They switched Falcons," she said.

"There was also something oddly familiar about the other pilot. Who was he?" I squinted at her.

"The other pilot was ..." Grandma looked away and back to me. "Teddy."

The room spun and my knees went weak. Kevin caught me right before I hit the wall. I took a wrong turn and was lost in his sea-green eyes for a second. "Thanks," I whispered.

He pushed me to my feet and kept his hand on my back. An exhilarating rush shuddered through my body the second he touched me. Just like our first meeting in Key West.

I shook it off and returned my attention to Grandma. "Teddy? Was here? Bu ... but why didn't he approach ..." I said.

"Rosie, it's not safe right now." She tilted her head. "I chewed him out for doing that. But he insisted on seeing his beautiful daughters." She cradled my face in her hands and gave me a kiss on each cheek. "That's from him," she said ruefully.

He left me all over again. A stabbing pain seared through my breastbone as if someone ripped my heart out and crushed it. I rubbed my chest, closed my eyes, and drew in deep breaths. *No crying, Rose.*

Kevin stood quietly by my side.

"What the hell is going on, Grandma. Please tell me," I pleaded.

"That is a story for ano—"

"*No.* It is a story for now. I know we don't have a lot of time but give me the condensed version. I need to know what I'm getting into," I demanded.

"Have a seat." She motioned to the sofa.

I plopped down and Kevin sat next to me.

CHAPTER 56

Grandma paced as she told me the truth. "You have to understand your father. He always had grass growing under his feet. I'm surprised he settled and had children. But once he met your mother, he was done. I saw it on his face." She looked at me with a loving expression.

"Your grandfather and I were faced with challenges when it came to raising our son. We lived overseas and moved every few years. We had no personal life and took turns with shopping, day care, and after-school activities. I even had secure lines at the house. Your dad grew up learning new cultures and languages. He would frequent art galleries and talk to the artists."

"That's how he came to love art so much," I

pondered out loud.

Grandma retrieved two of the Falcons from the safe room and leaned them against the wall, side by side. "He is quite the artist." She stood back, tilted her head, and smiled at them.

I bent down and examined them. I couldn't tell the difference. "He is good," I said. I don't know if I was impressed or disgusted.

As I stared into space, my thoughts ran a marathon. I flipped back to them. "Wait. If you and Grandpa were in the CIA, why has Teddy been on the run and avoiding his own family? Unless ..." I paced, gesturing my hands as if I were Sherlock Holmes solving a crime. "He's in the CIA too and you're his handler?" I stopped and stared with an *aha* look. After all these years I finally figured it out. I felt like an international woman of mystery who just solved the crime of the century.

She remained silent for what seemed like an eternity and sat next to Kevin. "Mostly true. Except Teddy was an agent, not an officer." She put her chin on her cane.

"You mean a spy?"

She sat back and nodded. "Mmm hmm. But I didn't handle him, it wasn't allowed. Lily's parents were, until they died in a plane crash."

"They were killed two years ago. Who has been dealing with him since?"

"Me. I was a go-between. Since I've been retired, I relayed the information."

Kevin stared at me. I could see the wheels spinning in his head too.

"But ... he was in prison for killing Max's

father. How could he work for you all?" I asked.

"Yes, he was. He received a reduced sentence for rolling over on cartel members. Teddy was no hardened criminal." She shot me a reassuring look. "You see, during his time in the federal system, he uncovered things that only the underworld was privy to, like targets of terrorisms, drug lords, and who was funding whom, etcetera.

"He was a patriot and didn't like what he was hearing, so he started sending his mother paintings." She waved her hands to the Falcons. "Encrypted information is beneath the paintings. Some proved to be useable, some not." She stared.

"Why use the Falcon?" I asked.

"He loved it so much, it reminded him of his family." She touched my arm. "So, he began memorizing every stroke. It became his signature over time. He would send other paintings as well, but once the Falcon came, I knew it was a message. Teddy became known to the dark underworld as the Ghost Artist. He was under the radar until recently. An old and trusted friend turned on him. For likes of a woman." She rolled her eyes.

"I heard rumblings of him, but I thought it was just a rumor. And you were the retired connection." Kevin stood up and ran his fingers through his hair.

"How could you let your son be involved in all this?" I asked.

"It was his choice. Now he is an asset. I'm sorry. We are inches from closing in on them,"

Grandma said.

"What information is under the painting that Max wants?" Kevin asked.

"That we need to save for later." She looked at her watch.

"One more question, does Max know of the family's affiliation with the CIA?" I asked.

"No. He's just some twisted son of a ... uh, er. S.O.B. Who apparently has a sick obsession with you." She smoothed my hair and kissed my forehead. "Please be careful, Rosie."

"I got this ... but won't Max know that neither is the original?"

"Let's hope not. Don't let him get that close." She pulled out two more Falcons from the safe room. "These are his best and have useless information. Take them."

I exhaled and nodded to Kevin.

"It's show time."

CHAPTER 57

Kevin and I drove in silence to the Ravalli County Sheriff's Office. I was on information overload and my head hurt. Who would have thought I came from a family of spies? I shucked it off as we pulled into the back lot.

It was ten-thirty when we walked into the crowded briefing room. Sheriff Scott Horton greeted me with a hearty handshake. He was a cheerful man with the essence of a rural Montana sheriff. Scott met Kevin's height and weight, with reddish-brown close-cropped hair and a matching horseshoe mustache and beard. He was dressed in full uniform and wore black Ariat boots, with a black felt cowboy hat.

I apologized for reigning terror on his town. He shot me a dimpled smile and his brown eyes crinkled when he laughed. Sheriff Horton thanked me for not going Jane Wayne and told me I was in excellent hands with his team. He was a hands-on kind of sheriff and would be there, too.

A half hour later, I pulled onto the tarmac, cut my head lights, but kept the engine running. The airport's building lights were on, so it was easier to see as I removed both paintings, placing them on Grandma's handheld cart. A fleeting thought shot through my mind. Was I was meeting with Shilo and not Max? Or worse yet, the nefarious characters who were after Teddy?

At this point, it didn't matter.

The wind picked up and snow flurries fell, a shiver cut through me. I zipped my coat and instantly regretted taking off the ballistic vest the sheriff loaned me. But if Max—I refused to call him Thomas—spied it, he would have known the entire Ravalli County Posse waited in the shadows.

As I approached the only plane on the runway, a Cessna 310, the runway lights suddenly illuminated. My body trembled. At first, I dismissed the tremors to the rapid drop in temperatures, but then I thought about my last encounter with Max. After I shot him and ran for my life, I was almost blown to smithereens.

I shrugged it off as I peered up to the cockpit. There was only one person in the plane, the pilot. He appeared to have a checklist of sorts in his hands, I surmised he was preparing for take-off. I've seen Tubbs perform the same pre-flight inspections.

"Hmm, where is he?" Just as the words passed my lips an Escalade drove on the tarmac and parked a few feet away from the plane.

The driver's window rolled down.

It was him.

My blood boiled and eyes narrowed. I thought about the unimaginable things I'd like to do to him.

I cleared my throat. "I like the new hair color, Sam, uh, I mean Max." I gave him a shit-eating grin.

"It's Thomas," he snapped. "Sammy, the weak little boy has ceased to exist, and Max, well, he has too many warrants." He snickered.

"Whatever." Damn, I'd hoped the mention of Sammy would poke the bear. Didn't work. "Where is Heidi?" I yelled.

He pulled a Glock 40 mm on me and jutted his chin behind him.

"I want to see her," I snarled.

Max rolled down the rear passenger window.

Heidi sat with her mouth gagged and hands tied behind her back. She wore a frantic look as the women's scarf muffled her cries.

Just then, the pilot approached. "Mr. M. We're re—" He stood frozen as Max held the gun on me.

The pilot caught me off guard. He was the perfect specimen of a man, tall, blond, with a chiseled face. It was too dark to see his eye color, but I imagined they were blue. He could've been on the cover of GQ Magazine.

"Hey." He looked at me. "I have nothing to do with any of this, I ... I'm just a pilot." He waved his hands in surrender to me.

"Shut the hell up, Dale, or I'll shoot you, too."

I turned my attention back to Heidi and attempted to flash a reassuring smile, but I couldn't forge one.

As I went to open her door, Max shouted, "Not so fast. I want to see the Falcons. But first show me you're not armed or wired." Max gestured with the Glock.

I unzipped my jacket, took it off, and shook it. "See." I smirked.

"I know you have a bra holster too." Max cocked his head.

I curled my frozen fingers and clenched my jaw. "Fine." I set the jacket down on the ground and pulled up my shirt to reveal a gun-less bra. "Nada!" I snapped.

"What the hell." Kevin chirped in my earpiece.

I glared, picked up my coat, and shrugged back into it.

"Look inside the boxes, Dale." Max jutted his chin.

"You don't trust me?" I sneered.

"*No*. The last time you gave me an acrylic piece of shit," Max snarled.

Dale pulled the paintings out, one at a time, and showed his boss.

Sweat dripped down my shirt. *What if he can tell?*

"Load them on the plane," Max demanded as he exited the SUV.

"Not so fast." I held my hands up to him. "Heidi first."

Before I opened the SUV's rear door, Dale snatched the cart and ushered the paintings away, loading them on the Cessna. I'd never seen anyone move so fast.

I quickly removed Heidi from the Escalade and untied her. A man's tie bound her wrists. By the looks of her restraints, Max wasn't prepared to kidnap anyone this trip.

Heidi squeezed me as tears fell down her face.

"Take my car and don't look back," I whispered in her ear.

She scurried off as Dale tossed the empty cart down and climbed the steps to the cockpit.

Max approached me, stuck the forty to my ribs, and drew closer to me.

My body quivered. I'd forgotten how tall he was. He had a good five inches on me.

"You and I are going to get reacquainted, my love." He smelled my hair and kissed my neck. "Now get in the plane," he snapped.

I furrowed my brows and jerked my head away from him. "That wasn't part of the deal. You told me the Falcons for Heidi."

"I lied." He smirked as he pushed me to the Cessna.

"Don't do it, Red! Step back, we're coming in," Kevin chirped in my ear again.

As I stepped aside, a black GMC emerged from behind a hangar. It approached us head on, the high beams blinded me. The driver's window rolled down. It was Shilo.

Max snatched my jacket, but I lowered my center of gravity and bolted backwards.

During my escape from Max's clutches, Dale started the left engine. That was Max's cue. He scampered up the steps on the right wing of the plane, looked back and shouted, "This is not over."

As Max stepped into the cabin, Shilo unloaded her pistol at me.

I dove to the ground and rolled as I retrieved my 9 mm shield from my ankle holster, taking cover by the SUV's engine block and fired back at Shilo.

The GMC swerved and hit a parked plane and caught fire. Shooting at or from a moving vehicle was forbidden in my department. At that moment, I did not care.

The deputies approached the tarmac with the red and blue lights flashing.

I turned my attention to the Cessna and watched Dale taxi down the runway as he started the right engine. With my adrenaline on high and out of instinct, I chased the plane and fired at it. Yeah, I'd watched too many action films. But unlike the movies, he got away. Sparks flew as my rounds ricocheted off the plane's wings. As Max reached out to close the cabin door, his arm flinched. He looked back and glared.

"I lied, too," I shouted breathlessly over the engine noise.

Max grabbed his arm and scowled, closing

the door.

The locals focused their attention on the ground. They extracted Shilo from her vehicle seconds before it was fully engulfed in flames.

I was lightheaded watching the Cessna's wheels leave the ground. As I cursed it, Kevin ran to me. "Rose ... are you okay?"

I whirled around to face him and felt a warm sensation trickle down my body.

"Oh, crap!" he yelled.

My knees went weak, and vision telescoped.

CHAPTER 58

I stirred to a blazing pain in my shoulder as a paramedic smiled upon me.

"Hello, Rose. My name is Teri, and I will be taking care of you. You're a lucky lady, it's just a flesh wound. A few stitches will fix you up, but you passed out for a couple minutes, so we are going to transport you to the hospital to have you checked out. Are you okay with that?"

"I ... I guess."

As Teri applied a pressure bandage, it occurred to me Heidi was injured too. "Wait, where is Heidi? She needs attention more than I do. Shilo chopped off her finger."

Heidi popped out from behind the ambulance door. "I'm fine." She wiggled all ten digits in front of me. "That crazy Shilo cut off her own finger. She knew Maxwell would have been furious if she hurt me."

"Oh, he does have a heart," I mumbled.

Forty-five minutes and six stitches later, my right arm hung in a sling. A few short months ago, I was shot in my left shoulder. I pondered the irony.

As I exited the trauma room, Kevin greeted me with a smile and gentle embrace.

"Have you been here the whole time?" I asked.

"Of course, Red. Do you think I was going to leave you alone?" He grinned and linked his arm in my good one.

"I can walk." I tried to pull away.

"I know, but you suffered a loss of blood." He lifted the bloody, holey jacket.

"Two jackets in two days. I'm on a roll. And this one is Lily's." I nodded to it.

"I don't think she'll care. As long as you're okay." He chuckled and shook his head.

"What's so funny, Agent O'Malley?" I elbowed him.

"Boy, James was right, you can be a stubborn brat." He clung tight to me.

As we strolled down the corridor of the ER and into the main hospital, it occurred to me that for the first time in months, a man's touch comforted me. James was the only person of the opposite sex I allowed to get this close to me. But he didn't count, since he was my brother.

Kevin, on the other hand, made my body tingle. I pulled away from him, but he wouldn't let go. I wasn't ready for intimacy but allowed it for the moment. After all, I was shot and weak-kneed.

He looked down and chuckled. Although he was just two and a half inches taller than me, I felt petite next to him.

"What now?"

"You kicked ass out there tonight. I loved the drop and roll as you drew your gun. Man, that was kinda sexy. But please don't ever lift your shirt again. Unless I'm close enough to see it." His cheeks grew rosy.

His flirtatiousness hung in the air for a minute. A moment too long. I turned away to hide my flushed face and neck and elbowed him in the gut, again.

"Oof." He let out an exaggerated puff of air. "Instead of Red, I think I'm going to call you Janie Bond." He pulled back and roared.

I rolled my eyes and snort laughed as he opened the door to my sister's hospital room.

The conversations stopped and everyone stared.

"Sorry, was I too loud?" I covered my mouth.

Laughter returned as they watched us.

Saki tilted her head to me like a curious puppy. I knew what she was thinking.

I stood at the threshold and took it all in.

James sat next to his wife and held her hand, while Heidi sat on the other side of Saki's bed. All three wore a peculiar grin.

Kaylee laid on the couch across from them, Tubbs by her side.

Out of nowhere, tears rolled down my cheek. I turned toward Kevin to hide my face.

He whispered in my ear. "It'll be our little secret," and gave me a wink.

I wiped my tears and scurried to Saki. I squeezed her and caressed her face like I did when she was a baby. "I am so sorry." I lowered my head in shame.

"It's okay, Felicity." James hugged me. "They're both fine."

I looked at Kaylee and back to Saki and smiled. "Yes, they are, thank God."

"Um ... Felicity. That's not the, *they* I was referring to." James glowed.

CHAPTER 59

"What?!" Tears formed, again.

"Sis, that's why I have been so moody and shi—" She covered her mouth. "I gotta stop swearing or this baby's first words will be bad ones," she said, rubbing her belly.

"But I thought the tests were negative." I tilted my head as I held her hand.

"There is an error rate." Saki laughed.

I hugged her so tight, again. I didn't want to let go.

Kevin gave James a congratulatory bro hug.

I looked around the room. "Hey, where's Grandma?"

"She and her crew returned to Darby. She knows." Saki sparkled. "Oh ... she wants you and Kevin back up there ... tonight. She'll be awake."

Kaylee chimed in. "So ... Max or Thomas or whoever, got away, again?"

"Whoa. Major déjà vu moment. Didn't we just have this same conversation in a hospital a few months ago?" Saki blurted and giggled.

We all silently shook our heads in unison, each most likely reflecting.

"He'll be taken into custody by the authorities in Kalispell." Kevin broke the silence. "I think your Grandma put a tracker on one of the Falcons."

"One?" Saki tilted her head.

I looked at Kevin with wide eyes and back to Saki. "Uh ... he meant the Falcon. Long story." I puffed my cheeks. It relieved me Tubbs was the only person who caught it.

Ugh, more secrets. This needed to end at some point. I sighed.

"What about Shilo? Is she ... dead?" Heidi sat up straight.

"No, they pulled her out and brought her here. She was medically cleared and is now in the local jail, with Maggie. They released Rebel. He turned on his sister. I guess he was tired of being bossed by the little monster," Kevin said.

Just then a petite nurse with short-reddish brown hair opened the door.

James laughed.

The nurse rolled her head and chuckled, "Oh boy. You are all a sight for sore eyes. Are you following me?" Scarlett asked.

I looked at her dumbfounded and cocked my head. "Do I know you?"

"I was your nurse in Sacramento." She peered at my shoulder." I see you haven't changed."

Scarlett told us she relocated to Montana for a simpler, quieter lifestyle. "You all didn't move here too, did you?" She pulled her head back and shot us questioning glances.

"Don't worry, you're safe," James replied.

"Okay." She laughed and was back to business. "Sorry folks, visiting hours have been over for a while."

"Aye, aye. Ms. Scarlett." James jumped to attention and saluted her.

"Oh, you stop. You silly man." Scarlett waved at him.

"Kevin and I will take off to Grandma's. I'll see you all later. Grandma made arrangements for us to stay at a local lodge. She knows a guy." I grinned. "Maybe we can start enjoying our trip." I gave Saki one last hug. "We've a lot to celebrate." I blew her a kiss.

As I headed to the door, I turned. James gazed into his wife's eyes and held her hand, talking about baby names. It occurred to me, my best friend, work partner, the AP to my Felicity, was now soon to be a father. It was time to let him go. I had to let them all go and start their lives in Florida.

My emotional pain and ferocity melted like honey. How can anyone be angry at this sight? I felt Bradley and Mom smile upon us ... closure? Check.

As I grabbed the door's handle, so did Kevin. Our eyes locked, and I quickly moved my hand away.

We walked out of the hospital in silence.

CHAPTER 60

It was just after one a.m. when we arrived at Grandma's and were famished. Kevin said his specialty was breakfast and offered to cook.

Jake sat with Lily on the couch, engaged in a close conversation. I noticed sparks between the two.

Griz snoozed on the floor by the fire with Brian and Stevo, all belly up and snoring.

While Kevin prepped the food, Grandma gave a Max update.

"When Max landed in Kalispell, the locals greeted him and arrested him under the name of Maxwell Ryan. Thomas Marchetti never officially existed. They'll hold him until the U.S. Marshals take custody of him." She read from her text message. "And apparently, he was wounded." Grandma shot me a Cheshire grin.

"What about Dale?" I asked.

"If he cooperates, they'll release him. I don't think he knew what he was getting into," Grandma said.

"For someone who is retired, you sure have the pulse on things." Kevin smirked at her over the stove.

"Speaking of pulse on things ..." I nodded for her to join me. As we meandered down the steps, I linked her arm in mine. "Where is our ... guest?" I whispered in her ear.

We plopped on the couch. "Rosie, sometimes you gotta do what you feel is right in your heart." She smiled and patted my hand. "Per your instructions, I told him to disappear and never resurface. I'm sure he and Crockett took off with one of Max's paintings."

"Huh? You let him steal it?" I asked.

"No. Titos and I chatted after the drugs wore off. Crockett owed Max a lot of money. So, in exchange, Crockett gave up a Rembrandt that belonged to his family. He vowed to get it back. Titos found out and blackmailed Crockett into giving him a percentage. Besides, with all federal and local charges, Max will be gone for a long time and won't miss it," Grandma said with a satisfied laugh.

"Wow ... good for them, I guess." I nodded. "Hey ... we never finished our earlier conversation. What is beneath the most recent Falcon?"

"Yes, I was curious about that too." Kevin wandered downstairs with French toast and strawberries."

"First, we eat." Grandma smiled.

The three of us inhaled our food in silence.

Finally, I pushed my plate away and folded my napkin. "Okay ... now please tell me." I spoke as if I were a child waiting for the ultimate Christmas gift.

Grandma opened her room within a room and nodded for Kevin to give her a hand.

He stepped inside and his mouth dropped. He stared at a piece of equipment that looked like a scope of sorts. And gazed back to Grandma. "Now you've piqued my curiosity. Why do you have X-ray radiography equipment?" He placed his hands on his hips.

"How do you know what this is, O'Malley?" I asked.

"I'm assigned to the FBI's Art Theft Task Force," he said to Grandma. "But you know that." He turned to me.

Grandma snickered. "Not for long ... I hear you are going to be transferred to a CIA/FBI joint terrorism task force." She threw him a side look.

"Uh ... yes, but ... that information is confidential." He furrowed his brows.

I threw my hands in the air.

"I make it my business to know things. It keeps me alive." She scrunched her nose and gave him a shoulder shrug. "Anyway, the information contained under the most recent Falcon is right up your alley." Grandma motioned for Kevin as he wheeled the x-ray machine into the living room.

I surveyed it. "I saw this on a television special. One of my many sleepless nights." I rolled my eyes. "They detected a lost Degas portrait with a similar scope."

"Yep, it's been used for many years to study famous works of art and to detect fraud, paintings under paintings, etcetera." Grandma peered under the scope. "Okay, here we go ..." She stood and stared. "Now, neither of you can unsee this."

We nodded in agreement.

Kevin was first. "*Oh, my god*. What the he—" He gasped as he covered his mouth. "Where did Teddy get this information?" He pointed to the painting and quickly peered back under the scope. "This is classified." Kevin ran his hands through his messy salt and pepper hair.

CHAPTER 61

"**W**hat am I looking at? The only name I recognize is Marchetti Enterprises. That's Max's company." I gazed at them with a blank stare.

"You are partially correct. It's a ghost corporation," Grandma said.

"Ghost?"

"A shell whose primary purpose is to shield the owner's identity and money. These corporations have no operations. Some wealthy art collectors use shell companies to hide the owner's identity. It's not wrong until they use it for tax evasion, fraud, money laundering, or terrorism. Billions are hidden in shell companies and offshore accounts," Kevin said as if he were conducting a lecture.

"I read about that in the Panama Papers," I

said.

"That's why the U.S will be banning the anonymity of shells next year," Kevin said.

"It's a dangerous business. Criminals like drug traffickers and those with terror ties move money around the world daily," Grandma said.

"So, money laundering? How does it work?" I leaned in with my hands on my knees as if watching a movie.

"The condensed version is you start with dirty money, buy a painting, then turn around and sell it. And you put that clean money into a shell company or offshore account. The money is cleaned from the sale of artwork. Drug lords and terrorists freely move money back and forth, often between two, three, or more shells to create a financial hall of mirrors before the funds reach their destination," Kevin said.

"So, they're funneling money into the art world. But can't the art sales be traced?" I asked.

"It used to be in the art world that auction houses, galleries, dealers, and so on worked under secrecy. An art advisor would represent both purchaser and seller. A purchaser won't ask who owns the art, the seller won't ask who is buying it, or the origin of their money. And the art advisor keeps the identities of both parties secret. Many times, the auction house would not ask. But that's changing. Stricter checks are done to verify buyers and intermediaries. It's a trickier business now," Grandma said.

I blew out a loud puff of air, sat back on the

couch and soaked in the information.

"A terrorist would create a chain of art advisors or representatives, many of these don't know who they represent or the extent of their involvement. The financial backers of Al Qaeda were uber wealthy and well-connected," Grandma said.

"Yep, the sale of art has been unregulated and anonymous. But earlier this year, the anti-money laundering legislation was introduced to help prevent money laundering and terror financing through the art market. It'll put an end to the secrecy and piss off many people," Kevin said.

"Okay, so what does Teddy know, and why is the CIA involved?" I asked.

"A couple of the shells under this painting." Grandma pointed to the most recent Falcon. "Have been on our radar for months. One is a drug lord and the other with terror connections. We need to cut off the financial head to avoid another 9/11," Grandma said with urgency.

"So, wait. Is Max involved in terror funding?" I frowned.

"I don't believe so. He unknowingly became a pawn in all this. He was just moving around stolen art pieces that were never recovered. And chatter was he was meeting with one of the cartel's representatives in Kalispell. A woman by the name of Chena. She's a lawyer and works for some dangerous people. Max is a valuable asset to them, he has connections all over the underbelly of the art world and is the best at hiding money," Grandma said.

"How did Teddy get this list?" I pointed to the Falcon.

"From an unnamed source with the auction houses. But I fear his cover may have been blown if Max knows," Grandma said.

"The only thing missing is the actual identities ... oh, and the routing numbers. But that's next to impossible." Kevin smirked.

Grandma said nothing and bit her nail.

"Are you serious?" I snapped my head in her direction.

"You've seen enough." She turned off the machine.

"Wait! Grandma, you have a tell. Teddy is not going after these names, is he?" I followed her. "Where did he fly to after he left here?"

"I don't know. He doesn't tell me until I receive a painting. It's safer that way."

CHAPTER 62

After a few minutes of silence, Grandma blurted, "Rosie, I've been meaning to ask you something. Why do you refer to your father as Teddy?"

That was Kevin's cue. I watched as he took the dishes upstairs.

"I was seven when Teddy disappeared from our lives. Do you realize that was *twenty-three* years ago?" I choked back a sob. "He failed to earn the title of *father*. You know he came to visit me when I was in the hospital in Florida ... disguised as an old man." I rolled my eyes. "But it didn't count. I was in a bloody coma. And then like that he disappeared ... again. I thought *Dad* was back in our lives for good. After his second disappearing act I found it easier to refer to him as Teddy," I said with a cold, detached tone.

Grandma made her way to a roll-top desk and pulled out a pink and blue photo album along with a thumb drive. She returned to the couch and handed them to me.

"I won't make excuses, but he didn't abandon you in the traditional sense. Your mother insisted he keep away from the family. And he did, just at a distance. He's always been here." She patted her heart. "Your father has been keeping tabs on you and your sister for years."

"What? Why would Mom do that?" I pulled my head back.

"For the family's safety. And she wanted you to have a normal childhood. She didn't want you girls growing up visiting him in prison," she said.

I sat and perused the photo album. "Oh my God!" I covered my mouth. "He was at every major event. Our college graduations. My academy ceremony. My wedding and Mom and Bradley's funerals." I cradled my face in my hands and sobbed. The dam burst, finally.

"I'm sorry it took so long for you to know. But your father made a promise to your mother. And he always kept to his word," she said.

"Really, Grandma? He impregnated another woman when he was still married to mom," I cried out loud.

"Not exactly. She filed for divorce immediately after they arrested him. Your parents agreed to that, it was for everyone's protection. And she was so angry when he got another woman pregnant. But she loved him, and he worshipped her." Grandma sat next to me and put her arm around me.

"So, she knew and never told us? Come to think of it, we were supposed to have a heart-to-heart, but the cancer took her away so fast ... and that's when the roses started showing up." I wiped my face and my eyes glazed over.

"It's a lot to take in, especially at this ungodly hour," she said.

I threw my head back against the couch and closed my eyes tight.

"What's next, Rose?" She stroked my hair.

"Not sure, Gran. I'm questioning everything. You know ... I thought I knew what I wanted to be when I grew up, but I sort of lost my compass. I've worn badges my whole life. Girl scouts, explorers ... parole agent. It's not only what I do but who I am."

"Yes, you do have a bit of a superhero complex." She curled her lips.

"Thanks to your son." I rolled my eyes and smiled.

"But ... there's life beyond your badge, Rose. It doesn't identify you. Family does."

I pondered Grandma's statement. I had this delusion that once the truth was out, I'd feel whole and complete. But there was a middle piece of the puzzle missing.

It hit me like a ton of bricks. I shot to my feet. "Grandma! I know what I need to do." I looked at her. "And you're going to help me."

It was time to step up and be the superhero

my father imprinted upon me.

CHAPTER 63

Max laid on his cot and stared at the ceiling of his fifteen-by-ten cell at the Kalispell jail. Ten days and the view hadn't changed. He felt along the bandage on his right forearm where Rose's bullet grazed him. Yet another reminder of her. Max was deep in thought about the most recent incident with Rose when the cell doors popped open. He flinched.

"Ryan, time to go. The feds are here. You're being transferred." A tall, lean, corrections officer waved at him.

Max stood. He nodded without saying a word and marched out of the jail cell. He was escorted to Central Control and handed a paper sack that contained the street clothes he wore during his arrest. Max clung to the bag containing his Prada jeans and matching grey wool long sleeve shirt, and Hoxton boots. He opened the bag and inhaled the leather scent from his Saint Laurent single breasted belted jacket, that now had a bullet hole in the right sleeve.

This was more like it. He sneered.

A few minutes later two U.S. Deputy Marshals greeted Max and presented his transfer documents to the jail clerk.

One marshal was an Irish battering ram of a man who towered at six feet six inches with a closely cropped, bright crimson tipped haircut. The other was half his size and did the talking.

"Turn around and place your hands against the wall," the shorter marshal ordered.

Without saying a word, Max slowly turned like an obedient inmate and placed his hands against the wall. He clenched his jaws and rolled his eyes and drew a deep meditative breath as the officer conducted a pat-down search. After his clothed body search, the deputy secured a belly chain with handcuffs attached to the sides around Max's waist and restrained him.

"Don't you need leg irons for this guy?" the jail's corrections officer asked.

"Not necessary." The crimsoned-haired marshal boomed in a deep voice as he ushered Max out the back door to a waiting bullet proof Ford Expedition.

Max turned to the driver, a blonde female, and gave her a nod as he was assisted into the rear passenger seat. As the heavy-laden doors slammed shut, Max jumped again. Ten days in hell was all he could handle.

A few minutes after they cleared the jail's sallyport, Max shifted to the refrigerator of a man.

"Thanks, D.O.G. Now get this crap off me."

D.O.G., whose birth name was Douglas O'Glosson, removed Max's restraints as ordered.

The driver looked in her review mirror. "Nice to see you, Max."

"Thanks, Lucy," he replied.

Max turned to the shorter marshal and jutted his chin. "Who's the new guy?"

"This is Bruno Brown. Chena sent him. Don't let his size fool you."

For the first time in months, a closed mouth smile crept to the corners of Max's mouth.

TO BE CONTINUED

AUTHOR'S NOTE

As a dog lover, I wanted to pay homage to my two fur babies, Saki and Rose. Instead of writing about dogs, I chose to bring them to the human world. Most of the characters in this story are loosely based on Saki's and Rose's K-9 friends. This story is dedicated to all present, past, and future fur babies. I hope you enjoy.

List of characters and their K-9 identities.

Rose

Saki

Kaylee

Titos

Lily

Jake

Rebel

Maggie

Griz

Dale

Chena

Shilo

Heidi

Fiona

Tubbs

Max, a lab mix,
was a childhood pet. Pic unavailable

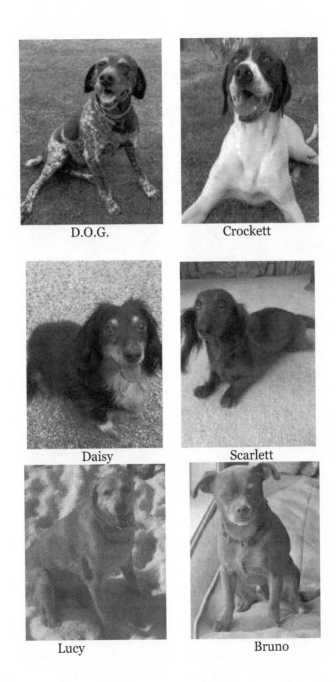

D.O.G.

Crockett

Daisy

Scarlett

Lucy

Bruno

Last, but not least, Grandma Lil, the only character based on an actual person. My mother-in-law, Lilian Weinstock was the inspiration behind Lil, and she is just as spunky as her fictional character.

ABOUT THE AUTHOR

S.S. Duskey retired from law enforcement with over 20 years of experience. She resides in the Bitterroot Mountains of Montana with her husband, Steve, and fur baby Rose. Rose and her late canine companion, Saki, are Sharon's inspirations for writing, not to mention her adventures throughout her career.

When she is not plotting mischief for her characters, Sharon enjoys spending time with her family, friends, and furry children in the outdoors of the beautiful Bitterroot.

Sharon invites you to contact her at ssduskey@yahoo.com or visit her website www.ssduskeyauthor.com. She can also be found at www.facebook.com/ssduskeyauthor.

Made in the USA
Columbia, SC
23 July 2021